# THE QUEST

# Q·VEST

# FOR HOPE

INVISIBLE BATTLES

## Book 1

# A. S. KING

(A SERVANT OF THE HIGH KING)

WRITTEN BY JENNY FULTON IN COLLABORATION WITH THE VISION
OF ERIC GRIFFIN (UNDER THE INSPIRATION OF THE HIGH KING)

ARCHWAY
PUBLISHING

Archway Publishing books may be ordered through booksellers or by contacting:

Archway Publishing
1663 Liberty Drive
Bloomington, IN 47403
www.archwaypublishing.com
1 (888) 242-5904

Because of the dynamic nature of the Internet, any web addresses or links contained in this book may have changed since publication and may no longer be valid. The views expressed in this work are solely those of the author and do not necessarily reflect the views of the publisher, and the publisher hereby disclaims any responsibility for them.

Any people depicted in stock imagery provided by Thinkstock are models, and such images are being used for illustrative purposes only.
Certain stock imagery © Thinkstock.

ISBN: 978-1-4808-2526-0 (sc)
ISBN: 978-1-4808-2527-7 (hc)
ISBN: 978-1-4808-2528-4 (e)

Library of Congress Control Number: 2016901558

Print information available on the last page.

Archway Publishing rev. date: 3/2/2016

# Contents

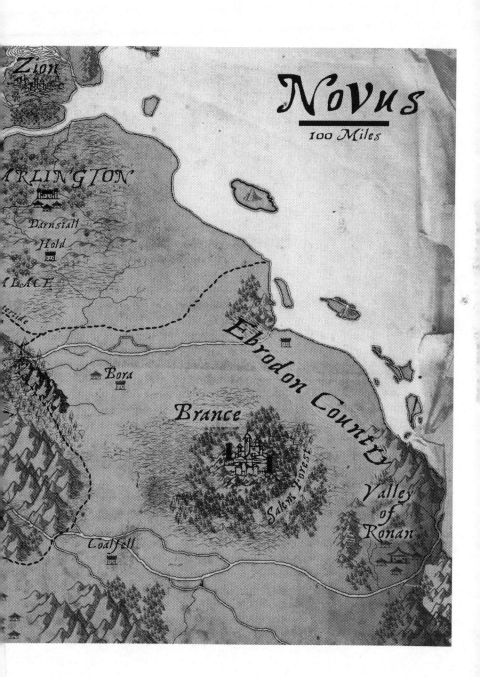

# PROLOGUE

Into the company of the crowded hall entered an Erela: a warrior, seemingly sculpted of diamonds—the many facets of his form catching the light and releasing it in dazzling patterns. He paused for a moment, facing the King and Queen of Novus who were seated on the raised dais at the far end of the room. Then, he began to move slowly and purposefully toward them. His dark eyes pierced deeply into their souls.

Once he arrived at the foot of the thrones, he spoke. It was a strong and powerful voice—a voice not easily ignored. "I, Zohar, Chief Commander of the High King, have come to you on his behalf. He knows of your worries and has sent me to ease your concerns." His tone became soothing, melodic. "The High King is concerned that this task He assigned you is simply too much for you to bear. I have requested, on your behalf, to be allowed to relieve you of some of that burden, so that your lives might be easier. In time, you will be better equipped for your new responsibilities. Until then, I have been tasked to share with you my wisdom and strength until you are ready to rule on your own. The High King did not mean to leave you so unprepared." Reaching into unseen folds of iridescent cloth, Zohar withdrew a small object. "As a token of my solidarity, I bring you this, the Gem of all Knowledge. With this in your possession, you will be able to serve and protect your people, especially, your daughter—"

The Queen let out a sharp breath and her eyes widened with longing.

Zohar gave her a kind, understanding smile, and focused the full force of his spirit on her alone. Very slowly, he held up his hand. The jewel sparkled, taunting her with its untapped beauty and power. Colors soared through the room in a mesmerizing kaleidoscope of light and shadow. "Come now," he whispered, offering the Gem up to her.

Malka, Queen of Novus, rose carefully and took a small step forward, scarcely aware of her action. The beauty of the Gem was hypnotizing and she found that she could not look away. Wisdom, he had promised. She would be able to better know how to serve those around her. Queen Malka moved to the end of the dias, stopping within reach of the gift. A hint of doubt crept in and she tore her gaze away long enough to look back for her husband's approval.

King Lev sat frozen, as though in a trance. Something did not ring true. He had heard of this—the Gem of all Knowledge—there was something he should know ... no. He fought to remember. What was it about this Gem? The High King had said to ... or not to ... not to what? King Lev shook his head. Something did not ring true—and yet his wife looked so hopeful. He should do something. He should—

Zohar's hand shot out and seized Malka's outstretched palm. The queen's eyes snapped back to connect with His. She was almost completely in his power, and yet, the choice had to be hers. Ever so slowly, he moved the Gem closer. Glancing back once more, Queen Malka beheld no movement from her husband, no indication that he was even aware of the situation. Very carefully, very consciously, she reached out with her free hand, and took hold of the Gem of All Knowledge.

The instant she made contact with the Gem, a rush of energy flowed through her being. A joyful, knowing smile lit up her face. She reached out to pull her husband nearer, to give him the opportunity to share in this wondrous gift. He did not get up. He did not take her hand.

She turned to look at him, still holding the wondrous gem. "My king, it's wonderful. All the knowledge we will ever need is within this jewel—I can feel it pulsing within me—Zohar speaks the truth; we will be able to better serve and protect our people with such knowledge. Come, take hold of it. Join me—" The Queen held up the jewel toward the King, enticing him to come forward.

Releasing the Queen's hand, Zohar watched carefully to see if Lev would respond to his wife's beckoning.

The King, finally seeming to come out of his trance, reluctantly stood up and stepped forward. He placed his hand on the gem—connecting himself to the knowledge it possessed. His eyes widen and, like his Queen's, his face lit with enlightenment.

Zohar, smiled and reached out to cover the King and Queen's hand which held the Gem. "And this is my real gift to you, your Majesties. May it bear much fruit." A second pulse of energy shot through the King and Queen. The thin veil of light Zohor had been wearing since his arrival dissipated. In its place was a darkness which radiated from him into the Gem and the surrounding hall.

The suddenness of the dark knowledge stunned them both. They realized, belatedly, that perhaps it was not wise to know everything all at once. The initial enlightenment they had experienced disappeared. Their faces fell. Joy gave way to pity, sorrow, disgust, shock, desperation, horror, despair … guilt. The Queen closed her eyes and shook her head violently as though to free herself of things she did not want to see. Unable to escape this knowledge by closing her eyes, she opened them again and reached frantically toward her husband. King Lev held his wife, but felt helpless to console her. What had they done?

A black fog swirled about them, and sprang out in every direction, like ink splayed across clean white paper. Dark thorns grew instantly out of potted flower basins. Once mild animals became fierce and stood with bristling hair, ready to attack. Slowly, yet with fearful persistence, the dark fog spread throughout all creation, devouring everything it touched. What once was good, was now broken.

Suddenly, as if another fog had been lifted, King Lev's memory returned. The Gem of all Knowledge was something the High King had promised to give them himself, a little at a time, once they had finished their training. They weren't supposed to receive all of it at once! And certainly, they weren't supposed to receive it from anyone else! How could they have forgotten something so important? He looked into the beseeching eyes of the woman he loved. Wide eyes full of remorse and uncertainty stared back. He knew he should find a way to lift her from the despair he saw encroaching in the corner of her eyes. He knew he should beseech the High King for forgiveness. As if reading his mind, Malka quivered her head back and forth. She was afraid, and so was he. They had no choice; their mistake was far too grave. King Lev took his Queen's hand, and a darkness that had gained a foothold within her latched more into them both.

"The High King will be furious with us," the tormented King whispered.

"Yes, there is no doubt that he will be," assured the glimmering Erela with gleeful confidence. "He will never again allow you back into his presence. What you were, has now been broken. It will always be this way, and there is nothing you can do to break the curse—" The deep tone was mocking and sharp with unbridled resentment. "But rest assured, I will protect you from his wrath. With me at your side, you will have no further need of the High King."

His last words, dripping with disdain, sent chills up their spines. King Lev wavered for just a moment before dropping his head in reluctant resignation.

"What would you have us do, Commander?"

"Call me." Zohar paused, and then spat sarcastically, "Call me the Dark One. As for my advice," he continued, "I highly recommend that you rid this kingdom of anyone who remains loyal to the High King. Those people must be utterly destroyed."

A hushed gasp ran through the crowded hall.

"Come now, don't look so horrified." The Dark One's voice took on a melodic note, hypnotizing nearly all who were in attendance, "After all, we can't have this kingdom divided now, can we? A divided kingdom—will surely fall."

\*\*\*

The pen paused in its labor. A white-haired man lifted his tired eyes from the parchment he had been focused on and directed his senses to scanning the environment around him. After a few moments, he shook his head and returned to his work.

"Grandpa," spoke a young boy softly, "What if they find us?"

"Oh, they will certainly find us," answered the older man calmly. He turned with an affectionate and understanding smile to look upon his young apprentice. "It is not a matter of if, but when, and when they do, you must do exactly as we have practiced."

"But what if I can't? What if I get scared and forget everything? What if my spirit isn't right?"

"All the what-ifs in the world cannot prepare you for the future. Instead trust and focus your thoughts on the High King. He is always watching, you are never alone. Remember what it is you have been and are being trained for. Think on the strength and power of the High King who has given you your abilities—"

A faint din sound interrupted the conversation, soft at first as the sound made its way through a long cave like tunnel. Gradually, the noise grew and shouts could be heard amid the clattering of armor and heavy boots.

"Quickly now," whispered the older man.

A few moments later, the door was thrown open. Human soldiers and towering Hellions, their distorted faces and monstrous figures casting eerie shadows on the walls, burst into the room, ready to seize and destroy anything in sight.

All they found was an empty table and two small chairs situated in the middle of a dark, dank room which had the appearance of being more of a cavern than anything else.

Howling with anger, the human leader cursed and hacked away at the only objects present on which he could vent his fury. The table and chairs were quickly reduced to a pile of scrap wood.

From a small hole in the corner, two small mice safely observed the proceedings without detection.

# 1

# THE LOYAL REMNANT

**Elsewhere in Novus**

In the southeastern corner of the land, beyond the darkened city of Zion, across the raging Teman River, past the rolling hills and sunlit plains of Alsta, over the treacherous mountains of the White Country and the flowering mountains of Ebrodon, is a place where members of nearly every race dwell together in peace and unity. Here, in the Valley of the Ronan, human Adamas, goblin-esque Yylecks, large apelike Zobeks, tree-esque Livids, giant Noroks, and goatlike Pronghorns all live and work side by side.

This all but unknown community rests safely sheltered from the presence of unwanted guests by a majestic mountain range to the north, a vast forest to the west, and a violent river that winds its way along the eastern and southern borders. With little need for strong, human-made defenses, this settlement is enclosed by a small stone wall that serves only to confine the livestock being raised within.

On a cool spring night, the wind whispered softly through the trees while the river roared in jubilant contentment. And in the undisturbed settlement, an invisible being slipped into the house of a peacefully slumbering couple.

*Ira, Ovadia,* spoke the unheard voice.

The man to whom the voice was directed awoke slowly and looked around. Though he could see nothing, he instantly knew who the visitor was and from whom he had been sent. "Forgive me," he moaned softly so not to disturb his wife. "It seems my second sight has not yet awoken."

He felt a smile arise from the spirit of the unseen figure. At the same time, he felt his wife stir beside him and was aware of her gradual return to consciousness.

After a few moments, their second sight was fully awake. A glorious, translucent figure stood before them. His head touched the ceiling. Powerful, shimmering wings were folded neatly against his back. His armour was smooth but majestic. His radiant form filled the small sleeping cell with numerous multicolored lights.

*Greetings, Melhem, chief commander of the High King.* Ira doubted his physical voice was alert enough to carry on much of a conversation, and he strongly suspected it would sound a bit rough if he did attempt to speak. Fortunately, his spirit-voice was sufficiently awake and able to communicate more coherently.

*To what do we owe this visit?* asked Ovadia, conveying a welcoming heart in spite of the lateness of the hour.

*The High King says the time is beginning.* Melhem's eyes lit up even more with excitement, and the light within him waxed even brighter, dancing joyfully against the walls as he relayed the words spoken by his master. *You have done well leading this settlement. Those under your guard have been learning and responding well. Now the time is near at hand for those outside this valley to hear the truth. They must be shown that which has been so well hidden from them for many years.*

*I would by no means disagree with the plans of the High King,* responded Ira, his brows furrowed in deep thought, *but how is such a thing to be accomplished? By now, those of us who live here are completely unknown to the rest of Novus. Why would anyone listen to strangers who suddenly appear out of nowhere? They would need—*

*Someone with whom they are acquainted,* finished Melhem, knowingly.

*Yes, and someone who can—*

*Unite them,* broke in the Erela again. He gazed sympathetically at the aging man. *Do not worry, Ira. The High King knows all these things.*

Ira's head bowed in shame. *After all these years and after all the stories from my father, I still forget. Please, though, who is this one of whom you speak?*

*One from the lineage of the Writer.*

"The girl." Ira's wife spoke aloud. It was clear her mind had grasped hold of the significance of the moment.

Ira, too, was struck by those simple words and the implications they carried. *Tell the High King I shall ready myself to leave immediately.* He moved as though to begin making preparations but was stopped as Melhem stretched out a halting hand.

*You will not be the one going. The High King has selected another to go—your young apprentice.*

"Levi?" Ira asked aloud, exchanging a doubtful look at his wife. *Do you really think he is ready?* He turned his eyes back to Melhem. All he saw, however, was the room exactly as it had appeared before they'd gone to bed that night. In the split second he looked at his wife, the Erela disappeared.

# 2

# DISCOVERY

While Ira and Ovadia discussed the implications of the message, a lone shadow moved silently through the morning darkness, making its way to the southern river. Once there, the shadow's form altered as it disappeared into the water and moved quickly and effortlessly to the island in the middle of converging rivers. The shadow changed again as it emerged onto the land and swiftly worked its way up the slopes of a small mountain. At the top, the shadow changed form once more, revealing the silhouette of a man of average height and build with light brown hair and dark brown eyes. Finding a place at the peak, he sat down—watching ... waiting ... looking to the east.

He was not disappointed. Before long, the song of sunrise began. Myriad colors burst across the sky. Everything around him lifted its voice in perfect harmony. The light began in the east and made its way across the land, chasing away the darkness of the night.

Levi breathed it all in, relishing the joy, the peace, and the new life flowing through him. His eyes lifted and caught sight of an eagle, soaring on the colors of the morning. With a slow smile, he reached his hands upward. His spirit lifted even higher until it connected to the essence of the eagle. Energy surged through him as he stood and raced to the edge of the mountain. With a great leap, Levi bounded into the air, his body taking on the form and characteristics of the eagle above him.

Now there were two eagles soaring among the clouds, flying free, exuding wordless homage to the great High King, the giver of all light and life.

By the time Levi returned to the small settlement, the morning work had begun.

"Hello, Celnar," he hollered up to the large Norok standing guard at the southern gate.

"Out again are we?" The Norok shook his head. His expression held a reprimand, but his voice was amiable. "It is a good thing it is only you who sneaks out past our watch and not something else sneaking in."

Levi smiled. It was the same response he received every day from the head watchman.

He continued on his way, jogging through the grazing grounds and gardens where Pronghorns were already busy tending to the fields. He waved a greeting as he passed and made his way to the work sheds that composed the next layer of this circular community. Not too much was happening there, yet, other than a few Zobeks going about, making sure each building had the materials needed for the day.

"Oof!" Levi collided headlong with something large and furry. He tumbled back, landing none too gently on his backside.

"So sorry! So, so sorry! Are you hurt? Let me look!"

Levi looked up to see a large Zobek head only inches from his own. The Zobek's eyes were very concerned. Levi smiled. "I'm okay, Awank." He brushed off the dirt. "It was my own fault for not watching where I was going."

Awenk helped him up, made sure he was okay, and then returned to his task. This reminded Levi that if he didn't hurry, he would be late for his own work.

He moved more carefully past the living quarters and finally arrived at the focal point of the community. He immediately began his work among the other members, helping to set up tables and chairs for breakfast near the small building that housed the kitchen. As they worked, young women passed by with pails of milk and water. Children arrived, walking slowly as they carefully concentrated on carrying baskets of eggs. Once their baskets made it safely to their destination, the children ran, skipped, and scampered about as they helped decorate the tables with handfuls of bright flowers. Savory smells from the kitchen made their way outside where they tickled the noses and teased the stomachs of all within the immediate vicinity. More than one eager stomach growled in response.

Before long, musicians set up around the perimeter of the breakfast area and began to play their call to breakfast. As the community finished their morning duties, they made their way to the central gathering place. Levi and several other men stood by to assist those who came through the line—helping mothers carry multiple trays for their young children, guiding the elderly and frail to a table before delivering trays of food to them, and attending to any other task of assistance that was needed. Once everyone else received their portions, these men went through the line and received their own.

Light conversation was interspersed with laughter as the community ate and joined their hearts, minds, and spirits to each other.

After breakfast ended and dishes were cleared away, it was time for lessons. Levi didn't think he would ever get over how spectacular and beautiful it was to see people from so many races sitting intermixed as they waited for the teaching to begin.

Once everyone was situated, Ira, Lead Servant of the community, stood, his bald head emerging from the seated group as he made his way to the wooden platform in the middle of the group. He wore simple workman's garb. His long, gray beard reached down to his small waist. In contrast to his diminutive frame, his voice was strong and firm. This morning, he spoke with a new excitement radiating through him.

"Today is the beginning of a new in our journey. For many years, we have been hiding, learning, and living secluded and protected. Our very existence is unknown by nearly all others. Today, that will begin to change. Some of you will be called on to stay, to continue learning, to continue the work that needs to be done in this community. Others will be called on for a different task. I will speak to each one individually on these matters. But first, let me remind you of the very beginning—of the one we serve and of the one who seeks to pull us away." Ira paused as he opened a weather worn scroll. All was silent as he began to read.

# 3

# In The Beginning

The narration of the events from the beginning, given by the High King to be passed on through the Erela, Melhem, to Raziela, a servant of the High King.

"There once was a darkness, thick and empty, with no purpose, no life.

"Into this void appeared a Light. It pierced through the waiting darkness—small at first, but then it grew ever brighter until no darkness remained. No one knows where it came from or from whence this life began. It simply was.

"This Light was a being, an infinite Being. He began to work carefully, purposefully—moving, gliding, and dancing through space in an intricate display. Exactly how long it took could not be said, for time was not yet an entity. Nor were space or solid objects. There was only light. Light was everywhere, and everything was light.

"Speaking with life and wisdom, this Being spoke into existence a glorious city—one that would glide through the heavens, a place from which his glory might dwell in fullness.

"Its beauty was only the beginning.

"Out from his heart, his hands, his words, he gathered the

light of the stars, mixing it with his own indescribable brightness. Wisdom poured forth as he fashioned the light into beautiful, crystalline beings. Their wings stretched out, iridescent, like rays of light. These creatures would be the reflection of his own brilliance and goodness. They were strong and would serve their master and purpose well. He called them Erela.

One of the Erela stood supreme above all the rest. He was stronger, more beautiful, and more brilliant than all the others—the epitome of splendor and radiance. He was appointed Chief Commander. His name, was Zohar."

Ira stopped reading and surveyed the crowd with a serious expression. "As most of you are aware, this Zohar is now known as the Dark One. He has nearly succeeded in erasing the name of the High King from the hearts and minds of those in this land. Now it is time for us to start reminding them; to awaken in them a knowledge of the one true King. As you go about your day—for we will proceed as usual until I am instructed to direct you otherwise—remember the High King. Think on the peace and freedom you have been able to dwell in for so long. This is what the High King desires for all his creation. You are now dismissed."

Hushed conversation was interspersed among the shufflings of feet as each person dispersed to their appointed tasks. Some tended to crops, some cared for the animals, some were artisans, blacksmiths, carpenters, weavers, tailors, scribes, guards, and watchmen. The children divided their time between learning the arts and sciences and being introduced to the various community trades.

Levi moved to take his place among the men and women who were being trained to receive "Second Sight." Before he had taken two steps, Ira's spirit stopped him and beckoned for him remain behind. Levi's gaze followed the group until they disappeared into the nearby forest. Then he returned his attention to the Lead Servant. His eyes communicated his question along with his spirit.

Ira approached the young man and looked deep into his eyes, searching for something. After a long silence, he nodded his head and spoke.

"The High King has a specific task that needs to be performed," he said in a low voice.

Levi took a deep breath and looked down. "You're leaving then?" he asked.

"No, I'm staying here. Levi, the High King has selected you for the task."

The eyes of the young Adama shot back up, holding a look of confusion and disbelief.

*Why me?* he spirit-spoke to Ira. *Surely there are other, more experienced transmogrifs.*

*Yes, there are,* agreed Ira, spirit-speaking in kind. *Nevertheless, the High King has requested you.*

*Do I have a choice?*

*You always have a choice.*

Levi nodded. *I will go. What is the task?*

*You must reach the Princess and bring her here.*

Levi paused and thought deeply about the request. *I have so many questions. How do I find her? If she is in the castle, how do I gain entrance? Once I gain entrance, how do I convince her to come? She has likely never even heard of the High King.*

*Fear not, my young apprentice, for the High King will guide you. He will go before you. In fact, he is already there.*

# 4

# THE HEIR

**3 Months Later; Earlington Castle**

Aliatta stood in an empty field. The sky was dark—there was no sun, no moon, and no stars. Nevertheless, she could perceive her environment easily. And what she perceived was frightening. Only a few paces before her stood a horrific creature which had plagued her dreams for weeks. It was like nothing she'd ever encountered in her waking hours, and yet, was unsettlingly familiar. Its body was a hulking, twisted mass of flesh and metal which towered several feet above her head. A shredded black cloak lay loosely over its shoulders, and one of its large claws held a long, jagged sword. Darkness was its covering, crushing every hint of light as it moved.

The monster snapped a drooling maw and growled.

Aliatta could feel its pointed anger radiating in her direction. She braced herself to flee, but found she could not move. Her feet were frozen to the ground. She tried to scream, but discovered her mouth was clenched in fear. A dizzying fog gripped her mind.

The creature curled its lips into a grotesque grin and stepped tauntingly towards her—its victim.

*It's just a dream,* she thought. *It's only a dream, like all the others. It has to be!*

*Help me!* she cried out with all of her inner being. *Oh, please! Someone see me! Help Me!*

Aliatta couldn't even close her eyes as the monster determinedly closed the distance between them. She could hear its footsteps, feel its foul breath. She began to quiver. This felt like so much more than a dream.

*Whoosh!*

A gale force nearly knocked her down as it rushed by, taking its place between the assailant and herself. Even in the intensity of the moment, Aliatta found herself noting the strangeness of the fact that she had felt no wind, only sensed it. A warmth spread through her body—releasing her from fear's bondage and allowing her to move again. The warmth spread to her mind and in another second she was able to clearly behold the unfolding scene.

A shining humanoid form with magnificent wings hovered before the nightmarish creature. Its appearance was that of iridescent crystal and its powerful wings beat as storm clouds. A cloak of red fell from the center of its wings and flowed out behind in the unfelt turbulence. Smooth intricate armor covered its chest, arms, and legs. On its breastplate was a prominent signet and it took Aliatta a few moments to realize that the signet did not belong to any of the families in Novus.

This new presence radiated a bright light which came forth from within and refracted out like a diamond in the sun. The nightmarish creature braced itself against the piercing light. It clenched its fists and growled, striving with all its might to move forward—confident that it could squelch this light as easily as it had the others. The confidence was grossly misplaced. With each powerful winged beat, the dark creature failed in its forward attempts and shied another step back—pushed by the gusts and stung by the light. Finally, with a furious shriek, it turned and fled.

The winged one settled softly on the ground, still splaying light all around. Then it turned and faced Aliatta. The full weight of its light settled on her as she cowered again in a completely different kind of fear.

*Why are you afraid?* it asked. *The Chashak is gone. The High King has heard your cry for help. He sent me to your aid.* The winged one spoke in rich, echoing tones. There was no human emotion in his voice, yet it was not cold. Rather, it conveyed a sense of comfort and peace. *The High King hears your voice, Aliatta,* he repeated. *You have been seeking the truth and have persisted, even under threat. You are not alone. The High King is gathering his people. He has not forgotten you.*

*Forgive me, sir …* Aliatta managed to stammer. *Who is the High King?*

The glistening man stared at her for a moment. His face contained no discernable expression when he spoke. *You have been given this glimpse into the other realm,* he said, *to give you encouragement and awaken your understanding. Your search is a right one. You will face many dangers and suffer much, and you must remember that the enemies you face do not exist only in physical form.*

*You mean that thing was real? Wait!* Aliatta began to feel herself waking up. A desperation for answers filled her and she spoke quickly, straining for every bit of clarity before it was too late. *Who is the High King? What do you mean he hears me? I've never spoken to him before!*

As the vision before her faded and all that remained was the light of the winged man, she was left with one final phrase.

*Continue to seek the High King, and you will never be alone.*

\*\*\*

Aliatta awakened to a face wet with tears. Her long dark hair was matted with sweat and tears, and heavy exhaustion clung to every part of her body. Clear blue eyes slowly took note of the pale moonlight streaming in through her lavish bedding drapery.

Doubtful that sleep would find her again that night, Aliatta arose and moved soundlessly on the smooth wooden floor to an elaborately carved desk. A few moments later, a small candle was glowing softly in the darkness. It illuminated the delicate face of the girl who sat staring absent-mindedly into the flame.

After several contemplative moments, the girl roused and took a habitually cautious glance around her room before reaching expertly into a hidden groove beneath the top of the desk. Exercising practiced care, she retrieved a small key and knelt on the floor. Her long, slender fingers glided along the floorboards until they found what they were looking for: a floorboard that moved slightly when probed by the right amount of pressure. A few more gentle maneuvers removed the floorboard altogether, revealing a small chest. She unlocked the chest and drew forth a crudely-bound collection of parchment. Without replacing the floorboard, the girl reseated herself in the chair and laid the collection gently on the desk.

In the comforting soft glow of the candlelight, the young Lady Aliatta of Earlington sat and contemplated all she had seen and heard. Then she selected a blank piece of parchment and began to write.

# 5

# LIFE FOR A PRINCESS

Aloud, persistent knocking brought our young writer to a less-than-desirable state of wakefulness. She reluctantly lifted her head at the interruption, and felt a searing pain in the back of her neck.

*I knew I shouldn't have fallen asleep at my desk*, she groaned. Her mind fought to regain full consciousness as warning bells began to pulse through her subconscious mind—*asleep at my desk ... my desk—the journal*. Her eyes shot open in alarm, her senses now fully engaged.

"Darling!" cooed a voice at the door.

The word itself was sweet and was sweetly spoken, and yet, something in that simple word sent shivers down Aliatta's spine.

"Are you awake, dear?"

The question was a veiled threat, one of which Aliatta was well aware. "Yes, yes, I'm awake!" the girl shouted in exasperation. She allowed herself to express an ample amount of annoyance. Who wouldn't be annoyed at having their precious sleep interrupted? Besides, it was far better to communicate annoyance than to raise suspicions with the panic she was feeling at a much greater level. She hastily shoved the parchment and chest back into the hidden

15

compartment, replaced the floorboard, hid the key, and threw herself onto the bed—not a moment too soon.

The door opened and a tall, elegant woman glided into the room. Long blond hair was intricately styled atop her head, encircled by a prominent crown. Black eyes contrasted abruptly with the softness of an otherwise delicate face. These eyes shot a disdainful glance at the girl who was slowly stirring upon her bed before moving to make a meticulous scan of the room with hawklike sharpness.

"My dear girl," spoke the woman. An inexplicable sense of coldness again punctuated the otherwise pleasantly spoken words. "Whatever are you doing still in bed? Your father and I have been waiting for you to come break the fast with us."

"You should have just started without me," grumbled Aliatta. "You *can* do that you know."

"I'll have none of your attitude, young lady." The practiced gentleness of the previous words disappeared, replaced by a harsh tone that brooked no argument. "You *will* be dressed and ready for breakfast in twenty minutes."

With that, the Duchess of Earlington turned and left the room, snapping her fingers impatiently on her way out. Two trembling maidservants instantly appeared.

Aliatta sighed and moved to do her mother's bidding, allowing the girls to assist with her wardrobe.

Exactly twenty minutes later, Aliatta stepped into the corridor and reluctantly headed to the breakfast hall.

As she walked through the long hallways and up the stairs, creatures of all races paused in their work to give her a fleeting glance before bowing in homage to her presence. The Lady Aliatta acknowledged them with a well-practiced nod, all the while thinking disdainfully about how pitiful they looked in their fear-shaken bows.

The breakfast hall was located near the top of an inner tower, high enough that it overlooked the outer walls of the castle. A large east facing window offered a breathtaking view. It called to Aliatta, inviting her to linger. She answered the summons willingly, resting her arms against the window sill. Muffled clatter from the busy city below rose up to meet her, but she cared not about the city, or the people who lived there. What held her attention at that window was the land beyond—high, grassy, uninhabited hills with large boulders thrown against each other in an erratic pattern across the land. Something about those hills called to her—made her wish she could fly out the window and dwell among them—

The faint hum of whispered voices interrupted her wistful thinking. She directed her full attention to the whispers, then took a couple of silent steps forward to better hear what was being said.

The first voice she heard belonged to her mother—a whispered agitation. "She won't be ready. You know she won't. All she does is laze about as though she hasn't a care in the world. The only thing she takes any interest at all in is that vulgar weapons training. The thought of one day being forced to bow down to her is … is … *intolerable!*"

The immense hatred contained in that last word hit Aliatta so forcefully that it caused her to take an involuntary step backward. What did her mother mean? Why the animosity?

It took several moments for the shock to subside to a more manageable level. When it did, Aliatta realized her father was speaking. "We have to tell her. She needs to know."

"Know what?" Aliatta stepped decisively into the room. "If you are going to talk about telling me something, you might as well just let me know what it is and get it over with."

Two pairs of dark eyes looked up in surprise. The Duchess seemed more than a little uncomfortable, but the Duke of Earlington looked squarely back at her with expressionless dark-brown eyes.

Without a glance at his wife, and without mincing words, he matter-of-factly said, "We haven't been raising you to be Duchess of Earlington. We have been raising you to be Queen of all the provinces within Novus—from the great city of Zion to the prosperous land of Alsta. You are the selected heir to the throne of Novus—the highest position in all the land."

"We should say we have been *trying* to raise you for that task," piped in the current Duchess of Earlington.

The Duchess then proceeded to launch into something which sounded rather lecture-ish, but Aliatta didn't hear a word of it. Her mind was busy elsewhere … *Queen of Novus* … *Queen of all Novus* … The words ran through her mind, searching for something to grab hold of, to connect to… Nothing. Her brows furrowed in confusion as she stood there, continuing to stare blankly at her father.

"Do you understand what I'm telling you, dear?"

Her mother's words finally broke through Aliatta's muddled thoughts and she shook her head. No, no she didn't understand what they were telling her. What did that even mean? It didn't make sense.

The Duke gave a long-suffering sigh and spoke very slowly. "You have been specially chosen, Aliatta, to become the Queen of this whole land. Your responsibilities will be immense, greater than you could ever imagine. In less than a year, on your 13th birthday, you will move to the capital city, to Zion, to finish your training under the King and Queen. Today, you will begin to assume more responsibilities. Your first area to supervise will be—"

"The dungeon," broke in the Duchess with a delighted gleam in her eyes.

Aliatta gave a disgusted grunt. The dungeon was her least favorite place, as her mother very well knew.

An hour later, Aliatta returned to her bedchamber to dress for her daily weapons training. Luxuriously alone in her refuge of peace, Aliatta's thoughts broke loose of their carefully locked cage and spiraled about in fearless abandon …

… I don't want to be queen … of anything.

*... why couldn't they have chosen someone else to be Queen of Novus, like my mother?*

*... do I have a choice?*

*... I most certainly do not want to go to Zion—the very name of the place sends shivers down my spine.*

*... what did my father mean about raising me—is that the way most parents speak of their children?*

*... why does my mother hate me so much?*

*... the differences between myself and my parents regarding our coloring and stature is rather strange.*

*... who is the High King?*

Aliatta tarried for as long as she dared, savoring the precious moments of pure solitude. Her only source of consolation was that her next event of the day was with the one person in the entire castle whom she felt she could trust. Maybe he could help bring sense and order to her tangled thoughts. Renewed with purpose, the reluctant heir apparent threw on a sturdy pair of clothing before carefully donning her leather breastplate—a gift from her trainer. It began high on her neck, moved over her shoulders, and stretched down over her hips. The craftsmanship was of the finest quality—multiple lightweight v-shaped layers of leather had been pieced together and highlighted with exquisite designs.

Now she was ready for training with Sir Raz the Calculating.

# 6

# Sir Raz the Calculating

"Good morning, your highness," greeted Sir Raz with a slight nod. His voice, like his clear blue eyes, was cold and unreadable. Unlike the others in the castle, he did not grovel at her presence.

*And no wonder,* Aliatta thought as she looked at him. It was doubtful that a man of his size and rank would have cause to grovel at anything. A well-crafted dark-brown leather breastplate that resembled scales made his already solid physique seem that much more imposing. The blue cloak he usually wore had already been carefully place on a nail next to the door. Leather greaves protected his legs, and a long, thin blade made of the strongest metal hung by his side. The weapon's smooth sides had been carefully etched with the intricate pattern indicative of a those used only by the highest ranked guards and given only to the country's greatest defenders.

Just as Sir Raz refused to grovel before her, so Lady Aliatta refused to tremble or be intimidated by him. "Good morning, Sir Raz," she answered in her standard condescending tone. "I do hope you have something at least moderately challenging for me today."

It was her usual greeting, but today her voice carried a hint of unrest. Sir Raz seemed to notice and he cocked an eyebrow in question as he stared down at her.

Aliatta quickly averted her eyes and turned her attention to the selection of swords. Perusing them with an expert eye, she settled on a smooth elegant blade which was perfect in size and weight. As with all of the selections, the signet of Earlington was engraved on its hilt.

With a toss of her head, Lady Aliatta dismissed the servants who were standing by to be of assistance, knowing they would go only as far as the other side of the door. Only after the door had closed firmly behind the last servant did she allow herself to relax.

Outwardly, Sir Raz appeared unchanged. His voice, however, was greatly softened when next he spoke. "Little Liat, I can see that something is troubling you. We will begin our lesson and as we work, I offer my ears as well as my instruction."

Aliatta nodded and her eyes filled with silent tears.

Over the next hour, Sir Raz led Aliatta through a combination of basic to challenging drills. The basic exercises came easily to her and she used these times to relate her dream and all she had learned that morning. Sir Raz listened as he'd promised, occasionally inserting a question or comment to clarify, but offering nothing else in response.

The lesson was nearing its end when Aliatta, beginning to grow fearful that she would come away from this lesson without having received any answers or counsel, stopped in the middle of one of the drills and plopped down on the floor with her arms and legs crossed.

"Well?" she demanded.

Sir Raz made a quick survey of the room and then positioned himself likewise on the floor in front of her. He took a small piece of parchment from one of his pockets and busied himself with it for a few minutes. When he finally looked up, Aliatta noticed an excitement in his eyes that she'd never witnessed before.

"You were visited by an Erela, Liat. In your dream he spoke to you and protected you. You have nothing to be afraid of. The High King knows who you are and where you are." He paused and looked at her carefully. His next words were spoken softly and with great caution. "I have been working on behalf of the High King for many years to look out for you and now it appears He is about to do something more."

"Wait, you *know* who the High King is? How do you know? How come I don't know? How come you've never told me? How—"

Aliatta's voice grew louder with her irritation and Raz clamped a hand over her mouth to silence her.

"Shh! Not so loud! It has for many years been forbidden to even speak the name of the High King. Doing so can land you in the dungeon, or worse. That is why I have never mentioned him. And even after this conversation, it is best to pretend that the only High King you know of is King Lev of Zion."

"But how do you know who He is?"

"A story for another time. For now, be obedient to the Duke and Duchess. Learn what you can. Don't worry about Zion. I don't know what He is going to do, but I have a feeling it will begin soon. In fact, I wouldn't be surprised if it has already started."

The door swung open abruptly as the Duke and Duchess marched into the room.

Sir Raz rose calmly to his feet and bowed his head, acknowledging their presence in the expected fashion.

"Taking a rest are we, Sir Raz?" spoke the Duke in a mocking tone. "I thought we had commanded you to *teach* our daughter. What can she learn by lounging about?"

"I am referred to by friends and enemies alike as Sir Raz the Calculating, am I not, my lords?"

"Indeed."

"Part of what is required for such a title is the ability to know the moves your opponents will make before they make them."

"I suppose, but what has that got to do with lazing about?"

Sir Raz handed him the paper he had busied himself with during his conversation with Aliatta.

On the paper was an intricate diagram of the types and angles of cuts, guards, and thrusts.

"The Lady Aliatta would do well to study this chart further," was Sir Raz's simple explanation of the drawing. To the lady, he gave a final bow of honor and a few simple words. "Good work, my lady," he said. "You are on the right track. Continue with the exercises we discussed. Do not lose heart in your training. It is clear that you were born to do great things."

The Duke grunted at the drawing and dismissed the knight with a toss of his head.

Sir Raz readily obeyed, casually retrieving his blue cloak from its place next to the door.

# 7

# The Dungeon

Distance wise, it was not far from the castle to the dungeon. The dungeon had, in fact, been built directly beneath the castle's rocky foundation. Mountain dwelling Skerps had, of course, done the work, bribed with the promise of being able to keep any valuable minerals they might find. This promise, like many of the other promises made in this land, had not been kept, and the creators of the underground labyrinth had been killed. Only one had been left alive on the condition that he guard and manage the dismal place.

In Aliatta's opinion, the passageway leading down to the dungeon wasn't much better. She trudged slowly along behind her parents, wrapping her arms around herself in an attempt to keep warm. The only light came from a few torches spaced far enough apart that the light from one barely touched another. With all her disgust, Aliatta walked proudly, displaying an aloof, confident air and desperately hoping her fear and disgust would not be evident. She absolutely refused to give her mother the satisfaction of knowing how much she would rather be anywhere else.

When she wasn't paying careful attention to where she was walking, Aliatta would look up to see how her parents were doing. The

Duke was whistled as he went along, casual as can be. The Duchess wasn't nearly as casual or graceful. She stumbled a couple of times, obviously more interested in spying out Aliatta's fear than in paying attention to her foot placement.

The trio finally arrived at the guard station where they were met by a very irritated Skerp: the guardian of the dungeon—Jixgaink Groundcash. His large, beady eyes narrowed in ill-concealed hatred. With obvious distain, he moved his short, sinewy form off the rock ledge where he had been reclining, into a semblance of the expected posture of homage.

"Aliatta, dear," spoke the Duchess in her smooth-as-honey voice. "You remember Jix. He is going to be leading our grand tour today and will train you in your future duties."

Aliatta gave a cold, condescending nod in Jix's direction.

He sneered and his abnormally large eyes took on an evil, mocking glint. "Let us get started then, milady. Mustn't keep the prisoners waiting." His voice was high and creaked like an old, scarcely used door.

The Duke chuckled. "That's what I love about you, Jix. Your humor is always, well—clean and fresh—unlike the rest of you. Lead on!"

Aliatta glanced at her mother and their eyes met. For a brief moment there was something they agreed upon—they both cringed as their noses involuntarily crinkled at the reminder of the Skerp's sour and repulsive smell.

The small group proceeded to make their way down the first passageway. The mugginess of the place, combined with Jix's rather strong odor, made the trip more than a little uncomfortable. Aliatta found herself withdrawing more and more with each passing moment. Her parents, with the exception of her mother's frequent sniffing of her perfumed handkerchief, were acting as though they were on a jaunt through the countryside, rather than being on the verge of descending into the depths of suffering.

"This is a good dungeon, it is." Jix began his "tutoring" session, his sour mood lifting as a trace of pride found its way into his squeaky voice. "Nobody has ever left, dead or alive. Oh, yes, it is a hopeless place!"

Soon they were passing the cells—small ten foot caves dug into the rocky ground, each barred by floor-to-ceiling metal gates. With each cell, the guard gave a short commentary, the Duke made a joke of the inhabitant's misfortune, and they all, except Aliatta, burst into laughter.

Aliatta tuned out as much of the conversation as she could. She didn't want to know who the prisoners were, what they had done, how they were being treated. She didn't want to hear her father's coarse jokes or her mother's lessons. She just wanted this part of the day to be over.

They were nearing the lowest part of the dungeon when a different kind of sound floated up to meet her. Aliatta's head jerked up in surprise, her senses on high-alert. After a few more steps, Aliatta realized that what she was hearing was singing. The voice was light, clear, and pure. The very air seemed to grow brighter as the music touched and enveloped her in a cocoon of peace.

The Duke and Duchess began to look slightly uncomfortable. Jix began fumbling in his explanations of the cells they were passing.

Aliatta began to pay attention.

"This, your highness, is where the most dangerous criminals are kept," stammered the guard as they approached the source of the singing.

"*She's* dangerous?" Aliatta scoffed openly, her eyes taking on shine. "Tell me please, what is so very dangerous about her? Does she enchant people with her song? Draw them to their deaths?"

"My dear," cooed the Duchess, with a slight tremor in her voice, "I'm sure I don't know who you are talking about. This dungeon certainly contains its share of *she's*."

"She, the woman who is singing," Aliatta was rather exasperated that her parents were pretending they didn't understand her. The song had been so clear. It couldn't have escaped their notice. She was alert enough now to catch and take note of the worried glances being exchanged between the three adults.

"You ... heard ... singing?" Jix's voice squeaked even more than usual.

"She is a mortal enemy of the King—and his Master," broke in the Duke. His voice was stern. All traces of his former humor had disappeared.

"I thought the King *was* the greatest Master of the land," challenged Aliatta. "Unless, of course, there is even more you have not told me."

"There is," he snapped back. "And you will one day stand in the presence of the true Master of this land. But today, know that the one you say you hear singing gave her allegiance to the enemy."

The singing stopped and a clear voice echoed off the walls of the otherwise dark and depressing place. "The High King is no enemy of King Lev. How could he hate one whom he created with such love?"

A shriek rent the air—a shriek that came not from the prisoner, but from the Duchess. "What is she doing still alive? She should be dead!"

At this point, the Duke, Duchess, and Jix all started yelling and arguing with each other, their voices crashing and colliding throughout the tunnels.

In the midst of it all, Aliatta heard the soft, but distinct voice of the woman, seeming to speak only to her.

*So, you have come at last, my little one. The time has indeed begun.*

*The time for what?* wondered the girl.

*The time for you to begin to know the truth—about yourself, about the High King, and about the Dark One who holds sway over this land.*

The gentle voice spoke no more and the voices of the three arguers finally ceased. They stalked back up to the guard station, not at all disturbed by the fact that they hadn't even finished their tour.

\*\*\*

The following day, Aliatta made her way to the dungeon for the mandated hours of management. She was to spend this time assigning food rations, delivering the food, assigning cells to new inmates, giving orders to have designated punishments carried out, and overseeing the disposal of dead bodies.

Aliatta, however, had other ideas as to how she would spend her time.

On her first day, she learned how Jixgaink Groundcash really spent *his* time. Like others of his race, his primary pleasure was in mining the earth for precious minerals. With Aliatta taking over the food delivery, he could now spend that much more time in his own, hidden tunnels.

So, she simply nodded that first day when he told her he would be busy with other engagements while she was there. Then she hastily disposed of the food to the appropriate prisoners and made her way down to where she had heard the singing.

Her excitement began to dwindle and nerves started to kick in as she drew near the woman's cell. She stopped short at the last corner which would bring her directly before the owner of the voice.

*What do I say? How do I begin? Why am I even here,* she worried. Aliatta had just decided to turn away and forget the whole thing when the woman in the cell spoke.

"Don't be afraid, child. Speak what you would."

The voice startled Aliatta, perhaps even more so since it had spoken aloud. "How did you know I was here?" she asked timidly.

"I felt your presence—and your footsteps echoed off the walls in a way very different from those of the jail guard. Come, let us speak face to face."

With a deep breath, Aliatta stepped around the corner.

# 8

# THE PRISONER

They stood there in silence, each gazing speechlessly at the other. Bright blue eyes stared wonderingly back at a matching pair of bright blue eyes. Their height would have been identical had not the prisoner acquired a bit of a stoop due to age and a number of years in captivity. Her long gray hair still held traces of black and it fell down to her waist in a tangled mass. As the prisoner gazed into the face of the young, richly dressed girl, her eyes took on a hint of longing. A wrinkled hand reached out through the iron bars as a single tear made its way down her crinkled cheek.

The movement took Aliatta by surprise and she responded with an uncertain step back. Was this the one who had been singing? How could such a clear voice belong to such an old woman?

The movement of the Princess had in turn startled the prisoner. She abruptly withdrew her hand, straightened to the extent she was able, and, with great effort, managed to collect herself.

"Forgive me, my lady," said the prisoner in the same clear voice she had spoken with the day before. "I forgot myself. You remind me so much of someone I once knew."

An unfamiliar feeling tingled within Aliatta. She discovered with a shock that she was actually feeling sorry for someone. This woman was strange in so many ways, and yet she felt inexplicably drawn to her.

After several more moments of surprisingly not uncomfortable silence, Aliatta found her voice. "I heard you speak to me yesterday, at least, I think you did. None of the others seemed to have heard you, but that could be because they were arguing so loudly."

"There are many ways of speaking, my lady. Using your vocal chords is merely one of them. Yes, I did speak to you, but more importantly, you heard and spoke back in the same manner."

"So, I spoke to you with my mind?"

"The words formulated there, but you communicated them through your spirit—a spirit that is seeking truth and light."

Confusion shone through the eyes of the young girl.

The prisoner smiled with understanding. "There is much you do not know—much that has been hidden from you—much that you are seeking."

"Tell me," Aliatta requested, and it was indeed a request rather than a brusque command of the kind she was accustomed to giving. "Please tell me, but first, tell me how you came to be here—how I can be sure I can trust you."

"I will indeed tell you my story, my lady, but the choice to trust me or not belongs to you."

"I came into being when I was fifteen years old, I believe. At least, that is the age the High King gave me. No, I wasn't born as you were, though I know you find it hard to comprehend. You see, at the beginning of this world, the High King created the first lives as though they had already been around for years. Some were made as babies, others children, and still others were brought into being as adults. Those first days were an enormous learning curve for everyone, especially the older ones!

"Each family on Novus was given a specific responsibility, something which would aid others in this land. My family was given the responsibility of assisting the Royal family of Novus, serving as their advisors and companions. Yes, I grew up in the household of King Lev, Queen Malka, and their daughter, Princess Elsie."

"Princess Elsie? I wasn't aware the King and Queen had a daughter."

The prisoner nodded and a smile lit up her face, transforming her features into a likeness of the carefree girl she had once been. "I was her handmaiden. We were great friends, she and I. We would run through the nearby forests together, climb trees, braid each other's hair—we were as close as I imagine any sisters could be. Elsie was very impulsive. She was impatient and eager to know and experience everything as fast as she could. I guess you could say I served to temper her wild spirit a bit, for I was far more cautious. As much as I enjoyed our exciting escapades, I actually preferred spending time with the Livids, learning from them as much as I could about the High King.

"And then, the Darkness arrived. I remember it as though it were yesterday."

Sorrow and deep pain filled the eyes of the older woman. Her features changed again to those of the weary, life-worn woman she now was. The next words came out in a broken fashion. Each one appeared to cause physical distress.

"On that night, the castle in Zion stood as a stark white contrast against the dark night sky. The skies above Novus had, in the beginning, been clear and blue. An incredible display of stars used to dance in the sky every night. For the past few months, however, that had not been the case. Thick grey clouds had covered the heavens, both during the day and the night. These clouds were so dark that the sun and the moon could not be seen. The only light came from momentary flashes of lightning-like brightness.

"On this particular night, we were all especially disturbed. The King and Queen were restlessly pacing back and forth on the balcony of the highest tower. They seemed to have sensed an unrest in their spirits and had apparently gone to look for comfort from the heavens. The sky, however, would provide them with no comfort on this night.

"Elsie and I had been quietly watching them and listening to their conversation from the Princess's bedchamber in a nearby tower.

"'I do not like this, Malka' we heard the King say. 'This covering in the heavens only appeared a few months ago and hasn't gone away since.'

"'Perhaps it is simply some new creation of the High King's,' suggested the Queen, though it was clear she didn't really believe that.

"'No, it is more than that,' the King replied. 'There has been silence from the High King since their appearance. I have to admit, dear, I'm worried.'

"'So am I. But surely, if there was truly something amiss, the High King would let us know. He would show us how to proceed and what to do for the people ... Darling, I don't know if I can do this—I get scared sometimes—I'm afraid I don't know how to be the caretaker He assigned me to be. Sometimes ... I just wish I knew more.' The Queen of Novus gave a soft sigh and leaned against the railing, staring thoughtfully into the heavens.

"The King approached and put his arm around her, as though to protect her. 'I do know what you mean,' he said. 'I often wonder if I am strong enough for this task. It almost makes you think the High King would have been better served by putting someone more powerful in charge of this land.'

"A blinding flash of light brought their conversation to an abrupt end. There was no warning. It lit up the entire sky in a blinding flash for just a moment and then disappeared."

# 9

# BETRAYAL

Then what happened?" Aliatta asked. She was sitting cross-legged on the dungeon floor, completely oblivious to anything outside the story being told.

"The huge flash of lighting-like brightness blinded us for only a few seconds. Elsie and I were stunned. As had become her practice, the Princess looked to me for assurance and guidance. I scarcely knew how to respond.

"'I don't know, Elsie,' I finally answered, 'I have a mixed feeling about the whole thing. On the one side, there is the sense of a great victory. On the other, there is a great foreboding, as though something terrible is going to come upon us.'

"'You're beginning to sound like those Livids you're always spending so much time with,' Elsie had teased with a slight smile.

"I assured her of my loyalty and friendship, but also acknowledged how much I enjoyed listening to the Livids and learning from them. 'They know so much,' I told her. 'I want to learn, too. I want to learn and write it down so others can know it as well!'

"Our conversation paused as we turned back to the window and noticed that the flashes in the heavens had stopped.

"Elsie was the first to notice the strange creature. 'What's that?' She asked as she pointed to the forests beyond the city walls.

"A dark shadow in the form of a man was moving slowly towards the city—towards us—blocking out any light as it went. After a while, we could no longer see it. The next thing we saw was a beautiful figure of light moving toward the city gate.

"'Open up,' the creature of beauty cried out. 'Open up, in the name of the High King! I have urgent business to discuss with the King and Queen!'

"The gateman gazed in wonder at the shimmering creature before him. He had likely never before seen such strength and beauty; none of us had. The gateman finally shook himself free of his awe long enough to fumblingly open the gate.

"The next thing we heard was the cry of a steward as he approached the King and Queen.

"'It is a messenger from the High King, my lord.' The steward spoke in an excited, halting fashion. 'He has approached the castle and requested an audience with you and the Queen. He says he comes with vital news from the High King!'

"'We will meet with him in the throne room,' replied the King, his voice shaking in anticipation.

"'Did you hear that?' Elsie had exulted. 'A message from the High King! We're finally going to know what has been going on!'

"The Princess jumped from her bed and was nearly out the door before she realized I wasn't following her.

"'Well …?' she prodded, looking back.

"'Well, what?' I asked. I hadn't moved an inch and had absolutely no intention of doing so.

"'Aren't you coming?'

"I shook my head. 'Something doesn't feel right.' I told her. 'If the message is so urgent, why didn't the High King come Himself? Besides, we haven't been summoned.' I had hoped this final reason would settle it. The Princess did, in fact, seem to be very nearly swayed into listening. Her impatience and curiosity, however, soon took over and she shook her head as though to shake herself free of the conviction that she may not be acting in a right manner.

"'I'll sneak in,' was her reply. 'They'll never know I was there.'

"Then she was gone.

"As for me, I continued to stare up into the sky, wishing I could rid myself of the feeling that something was horribly wrong.

"I learned later, from my father, that Elsie had crept quietly into the throne room and hidden behind a large tapestry on the side, close enough to the thrones that she could hear what was being said. The eyes of one of the figures on the tapestry had been altered on a previous visit in order to provide her with a subtle peep hole. From here, she could safely watch and listen without detection, as she had already done on a number of other occasions.

"She glanced around and caught the eye of Avinoam, my father and the King's Chief Advisor. He had shaken his head in disapproval at her presence and then returned his attention to the proceedings at hand.

"The beautiful creature we had seen soon entered the room and when he did, Elsie, along with everyone else, couldn't take her eyes from him. She finally tore them away and looked at her parents. They were clearly enthralled. Her gaze wandered around the room and then settled once again on my father. His expression was troubled. He seemed to be the only one in the hall who wasn't entirely pleased with this visit.

"The Princess was witness to all the horror which happened that day. She watched as the towering creature took a shimmering jewel and with it, baited her mother, preying on her insecurities. She watched as her mother stepped forward to take hold of it, then stood powerless as the Queen received from the Gem the knowledge of all that is good. She saw her mother reach for her father, the King, saying something and holding the Gem up for him to take hold of it. When the King finally stepped forward to join her, the creature laid his hands on top of her parents' hands. With their hands trapped within his, he released an unrecoverable darkness which would ensnare her parents and all of existence forever. The evil knowledge drained them and began to fill them with an oppressive darkness. Moments later her father remembered full well that this was the Gem which the High King had instructed them to stay away from. Elsie witnessed all of this and was deeply distressed by it.

"She raced back to her bedchamber as soon as she could, stormed into the room, and related the events to me.

"'What happened?' she vented. Tears ran down her delicate face, giving evidence to the storm of emotions raging within her. 'What happened to my parents? The darkness, the look in their eyes—I don't even recognize them with all the darkness. Why didn't the High King step in? How could He have lost track of one of His own creations? Why did He allow such a thing to happen? I hate this Dark One for what he has done and … and I hate the High King for not stopping him.'

"At this point, my friend stopped short. I had been listening so sympathetically throughout the narrative, but I could not contain my look of censure when she recounted her newfound hatred for the High King.

"'Well I do hate Him!' she screamed defiantly 'and nothing you can say is going to change my mind! You weren't there! If you were, you wouldn't be giving me that look!'

"I continued to stare silently at my friend, my eyes and spirit pleading with her but my mouth saying nothing.

"Elsie calmed, but only for a moment. When she next spoke, her voice held none of the rage, but rather, a dark determination. 'I have to leave. I will not follow that Dark One and no, I won't follow the High King either. Come with me, please? We can look after one another.'

"I begged her to stay, tried to convince her that the High King could explain what had happened.

"But she stubbornly shook her head. 'Are you coming or not?' she asked one final time.

"With a sigh of sorrow and resignation, it was my turn to shake my head. 'I will wait for the High King,' I answered with equal resolve.

"Without another word, Princess Elsie of Novus grabbed some of her belongings, stuffed them into a bag, and ran out the door.

"I have neither seen nor heard from her since that moment."

"Is that why the King and Queen had to choose an heir for the kingdom?" asked Aliatta softly. Her voice seemed to startle the woman who had apparently forgotten her little audience.

"I suppose that makes sense," the prisoner acknowledged.

"Do you ... do you know why they chose me?" Aliatta spoke slowly, not entirely sure she really wanted to know the answer.

The prisoner looked deep into Aliatta's eyes. The nod she gave was scarcely visible. For a long moment, she was silent. Her voice, when she spoke, was a gentle whisper. "That, my child, is a story for another day."

Aliatta stood to her feet and turned to leave. Then she turned back. "I have one more question, at least for right now," she said. "What happened to you – after the Princess left?"

"The first order given by the Dark One was to destroy all loyal followers of the High King. He must have thought that if he could rid the land of those who loved the High King, then he could have complete control and complete revenge.

"I was unaware of this and may have been among the first to be captured had not an Erela, a true Erela of light, begun to materialize next to the bed where Elsie had recently stood. 'It is time for you to leave also,' it told me.

"'Have you been here the whole time?' I asked.

"The Erela nodded.

"'Then why …?'

"'Why didn't I answer Elsie? I tried. Her heart had already set itself against the High King, and so she couldn't hear me. But come, there will be more time for questions later. Right now, we must leave.'

"'My father?' I asked.

"'We will meet up with him soon,' it assured me.

"The purge didn't happen all at once. It was a slow, steady, systematic process. My parents and I were among the first to leave, ushered out by a host of protective Erela. We took refuge in the Qatan forest, just west of the city. Protected from the view of our enemies by an invisible wall, we spent our days learning about the High King. The Erela were our teachers. Throughout the following weeks, the bravest of the group would regularly venture back into the city in order to bring out others who were resisting the continually tightening grip of evil and darkness. It was heartbreaking to see the city I had grown to love so much descend into such a hopeless state. There is one thing, above all else, that has helped me hold on to the hope that Zion will once again shine bright."

"What is that?" asked Aliatta, thoroughly enraptured by the story.

The prisoner looked intensely into Aliatta's eyes as she spoke. "The High King promised me that one day, one of my descendants would help usher in a new age of light."

Footsteps sounded in the dungeon corridor, alerting them to the return of Jixgaink Groundcash and bringing any further conversation to a direct halt.

Throughout the following days, Aliatta continued to visit the older woman in the dungeon. Each day, the woman would describe a different characteristic of the High King, giving examples and application from palace life. The two would also talk about the dungeon. The prisoner would suggest improvements and Aliatta would implement them. In this way, a task which had begun as a drudgery became an opportunity for fellowship and growth. You might even say there were times when Aliatta actually enjoyed herself, with the exception of the duties that required her to oversee the carrying out of punishments and the disposal of bodies. Those were two aspects of the job in which she never could get over her disgust.

After a couple of weeks in this manner, the day arrived when Aliatta went down for one last visit with the prisoner.

"My tutor is returning, you see, and I am being required to return to my regular studies. I'm afraid I won't have as much time to talk with you."

The prisoner nodded in understanding and the two grasped hands in a bond of trust and fellowship.

Lady Aliatta turned to go and then paused, struck by a sudden thought. "What is your name?" she asked the prisoner.

"My name, my lady, is Raziela. In some places, I am known simply as The Writer."

# 10

# THE TUTOR

From a strictly physical perspective, the hallways of the castle were much nicer than the tunnels of the dungeon. Sunlight streamed in through each of the many windows, offering light, warmth, and a stunning view of the outside world. Colorful tapestries lined the walls in those sections where windows were absent. Yes, the halls of the main castle were infinitely preferable to the colorless, cold passageways of the dungeon caves—or should have been.

To Aliatta, however, there was something now missing from the splendor of the palace. She felt inexplicably empty after having left the presence of the strange woman whom she now knew as Raziela. She had never enjoyed the sessions with her livid tutor, Torin Spring. He was a scrawny, sickly-looking, groveling tree-creature whose voice, when he lectured, could never seem to stretch beyond that of a monotone. Now, having experienced from a mere prisoner what real teaching was like, she was especially resentful of the fact that she must now receive such inferior instruction from such an inferior being.

It was, then, with a great amount of annoyance that Aliatta sulkily stalked into the classroom to begin her mandatory time of lecture from the wilty willow. *I'm not even going to look at him,* she determined as she slumped into her seat and threw her head down onto her arms. She expected a reprimand, or at the very least, his standard groveling greeting. When a minute ticked by without either, she began to grow curious. Another minute of silence brought her head reluctantly up.

The Livid was watching her with a curious expression. His eyes, though the same muddy color as usual, contained a brightness she had never seen.

She returned his silent bright stare with a fierce glare.

"Good afternoon, my lady," greeted the tutor, completely unfazed by her disdain. His voice had lost its usual monotone. Instead, it rustled quickly and softly, as you might imagine a short, gentle breeze would sound if it were to speak. It was also uncommonly cheerful and contained a slight trace of amusement.

The voice startled Aliatta even more than the eyes had. She took a closer look at her tutor. The size and coloring were those of Torin Spring, but there was definitely something different.

"Allow me to introduce myself," spoke the Livid who looked so much like her regular tutor but apparently wasn't. "My name is Teague Sunray. I'm Torin Spring's cousin. My cousin decided to prolong his vacation and asked me to temporarily fill in for him. Ah, I see you are confused. That is certainly understandable. We look enough alike that it is not the first time people have confused me with him. Now, shall we begin your lesson?"

Aliatta nodded dumbly, not quite sure how to respond to this change. This new tutor spoke in a quick staccato that was so very different than the slow drone of her former tutor. She wasn't, at the moment, convinced this new voice would be any more of a pleasure to listen to than the last one.

"Let's see, what were you last studying with that cousin of mine?"

The girl's slow answer contrasted sharply with the rapid pace of her tutor's speech. "Well … he was … umm … was talking about the kinds of plants from the forest where he lives."

"Oh, very good. That may come in handy someday. What else?"

"The useful attributes of each of the races and how they can best be put to work around the kingdom?"

"Is that a statement about what you've been learning, my lady, or a question?"

"A statement, I guess. There just seems to be something not quite fair about evaluating a group of people based wholly on how you can force them to use their strengths to benefit your own ends."

The tutor looked long and hard at her. There was a slight smile and a glimmer of approval in his eyes. His words, however, came as a challenge. "That is a rather astute and unusual opinion for a girl in your position to hold. As future Queen of Novus, don't you want to know how to rule over your subjects?"

"First of all, I don't want to be Queen!" A fire had been added to Aliatta's initial resentment of her required presence, though she was now at least interested in … *whatever* was happening. Her next words were equally fervent. "Secondly, it seems there has to be a better way of ruling than always forcing your subjects into doing things against their will!"

Teague's eyes were first thoughtful, then resolute. "I'm going to tell you a story, my lady—a story about these races. You see, they were all formed from the same seemingly insignificant substance: the dirt. The One who made them is able to transform what you and I might deem to be normal and unimportant into something very special. From this ordinary dirt, He formed the Yylecks, Zobeks, Noroks, Livids, Pronghorns, and finally, the Adamas. Into each creation, He breathed His breath of life. To each race, He selected kings and queens, dukes and duchesses who would be caretakers of those around them. Days He spent with each leader, teaching them a trade and instructing them with the beginnings of knowledge and wisdom.

"The Yylecks, with their pointy ears keen of hearing, sharp noses with no sense of smell, small bodies and lithe limbs, were shown how to discover precious metals hidden deep within the earth. They would be able to form these substances into items of use for each other and for the other races.

"Zobeks and the Noroks, as you know, are large and strong of body. To them was given the skill of builders and craftsmen.

"To the Livids, the wisest of the races, was given the task of receiving and teaching Truth.

"The Pronghorns, with their varying combination of human and animal characteristics, were entrusted with growing and tending to the crops.

"The Adamas were given the responsibilities of ruling, managing, nurturing and being the representation of the One who made them to the rest of His creation.

"Each member of each race held within them the desire to do what they were created to do. If they served their Maker and each other, these deep, inner desires would be fulfilled—their life would hold meaning and purpose and nobody in the community would be lacking in anything. If, however, they chose to pursue their own ends and purposes—if they rejected the gifts they had been given—then they would always feel that something was missing. Society would fall apart, and the strong would prey upon the weak."

Aliatta was silent, not sure how to take this new information or what to do with it. Then she had a thought. "Tutor," she said, 'you forgot two of the races. What about the Skerps and Hellions?"

"When a dark power began to exert his influence over the land, it emboldened some of the Yylecks to leave the path of their Maker. Their greed came to the forefront. They believed themselves to be obtaining the freedom to follow their own ends, but the reality is, in pursing their greed, they put themselves in bondage to it and by extension, in bondage to the dark power. These creatures soon became known as Skerps.

"As for the Hellions, the dark power had long been jealous of the Maker. His entire existence became focused on proving himself to be better and stronger than the One who created him. In an attempt to copy the creative genius of the Maker, he brought forth another race: the Hellions. Their forms, far from being beautiful, were ugly and warped. They were made to serve the dark power and a deep seated hatred for the Adamas was burned into their being. These creature now serve as henchmen to this darkness, loyal only to him, though otherwise, they seem to prefer keeping to themselves in the darkness."

The remainder of this session, as well as many of those that followed, was spent learning more about each of the races: where they lived, what they needed to survive, what their preferences were, how to best communicate with them, and what they were capable of becoming.

Aliatta ate up the information she learned each day, mulling over much of what her tutor said. During her precious moments of solitude, she would record as much as she could remember in her hidden journal.

# 11

# TEAGUE SUNRAY

While Aliatta found her mind busy with information after each session, Teague Sunray was busy with other matters.

At first he simply wandered about the streets, becoming familiar with the city, continually communicating with the High King about where he should go. These walks were not exactly pleasurable for the Livid. It pained him to see Zobeks and Noroks working in the shops with an iron chain about their ankle. It hurt him to see the wealthier Adamas disdainfully pushing aside poorly-dressed Adamas as they walked or rode their horses along the roads. He didn't want to see all that was happening around him, yet he knew he must keep his eyes open.

Occasionally, something about a particular person would give him pause. Their eyes would meet and a nod of understanding would pass between them. Teague would thereafter begin to observe more carefully these few people—how and where they lived, where they worked, what their habits were, what they had in their window, and especially, what they looked like in "Second Sight."

And so it was that one evening, about a fortnight after his arrival in Earlington, Teague Sunray stood before a small, insignificant wooden house which lay on the northern outskirts of the city. A pure white candle glowed welcomingly in the window. He could hear the low murmur of comfortable conversation, occasionally punctuated by the sounds of children's voices. Taking a deep breath, Teague approached the door and knocked.

There was instant silence. After a few minutes, the door slowly opened and Teague was met by a tall Adama with thick grey hair. Both men stood in silence, each studying the other closely.

Finally, the older man spoke, his tone low and his words very deliberate. "May the King live forever," he said.

Teague nodded, never losing eye contact. "And His light never be extinguished."

The grey-haired man let out his breath and smiled. Opening the door wider, he welcomed the Livid into his home.

Every day for the next week, as soon as the tutoring session was over, Teague made his usual rounds about the city and then ultimately found his way to this same home. He was very careful to keep a low profile around the castle. Since he looked so very much like Torin Spring and spoke to no one, almost everyone assumed that he was Torin. Teague opted not to inform them of their error and went about his business without interference.

There were, however, a couple of people who seemed to suspect something.

Teague sometimes caught Aliatta's weapons trainer looking at him curiously. Teague would smile and try to spirit-speak to him. *Everything is fine. Don't worry,* he said over and over again.

Sir Raz, however, had lived alone for so long in the midst of a dark system that he was out of practice in hearing the subtle communications of the light. He would glare suspiciously at the Livid and then walk away with his blue cloak trailing behind.

One clear, sunny day, as Sir Raz and Lady Aliatta were working through some basic fencing maneuvers, Sir Raz brought up the subject of the tutor.

"There is something strange about him—something different. I don't know if I quite trust that Livid, Aliatta."

Aliatta shot a puzzled glance at her trainer but otherwise kept her concentration on the exercise. Her response was made in a casual, matter-of-fact manner. "Teague Sunray? Why ever not? He is far more interesting than his cousin, Torin. He's been teaching me all kinds of things about—"

Sir Raz came to a sudden standstill and barely managed to avoid getting a rapier in the face. "You mean he's not Torin? I knew something was off! Why keep it such a secret?"

Aliatta rolled her eyes. "He hasn't kept it a secret. He told me right away. En garde, Sir Raz. You've lost your focus and are about to lose your weapon as well."

They continued to duel, but Sir Raz's mind was indeed no longer focused on the training session. Shortly thereafter, Aliatta succeeded in disarming him.

As they cooled down and their session came to a close, a soft breeze blew in, drawing their attention to the open window. Sir Raz glanced out and caught a glimpse of the tutor gliding quickly through the streets.

"I wonder where it is he goes …" he muttered softly.

Aliatta caught the words and her head tilted slightly in thought. Then her eyes brightened. "I'm going to find out," she said with a mischievous smile. Before Sir Raz had a chance to reply, the girl was gone.

Unbeknownst to Sir Raz and Aliatta, and unobserved by all others in the castle, two Erela had been listening in on the conversation.

*This all would have been so much easier had Sir Raz known how to communicate with our King's servant,* said one of them to the other.

*Don't be too hard on the man. He has served long and hard in this dark place for the sake of the Master. He has done what he's had to in order to survive and although he doesn't recognize it as such, he does hear from and respond to the High King to the extent he is able. The seed he has planted within Aliatta is a good one. We must now be about the task of protecting the girl.*

*A cloud. We are to surround her with a cloud.*

The other Erela nodded, acknowledging the direction given by the High King.

The next day, Aliatta pretended to leave the tutoring session in the same manner as she always did. This time, however, she hid behind one of the statues in the hall and watched as Teague Sunray left the room. She was more than a little disappointed when he went directly to his own chambers. Nonetheless, she refused to give up. Determined to wait him out, she sat down around the corner, expecting to be spotted at any moment and forced to return to her own daily routine. However, nobody bothered her. In fact, everyone walked right on by as though she didn't even exist.

After about an hour, her patience was rewarded. The door opened and the Livid appeared. Looking about in all directions, the tutor made his way purposefully out of the castle. Aliatta immediately jumped up and followed him, her heart pounding in anticipation of an adventure.

The streets were thick with people yelling, pushing, and clambering to and fro about their business. The sounds which had once been a meaningless, muted reminder of life outside the castle now slammed full force into the young, sheltered princess. As they neared the marketplace, the chaos of the city grew even worse. Teague moved with confidence in and out through the crowds while Aliatta wearily followed, doing her best not to get stepped on or jostled too much, frustrated that nobody was moving out her way. Truth be told, she was rather affronted that no one was taking any notice of her at all. Were they too dense to realize that the Lady Aliatta was walking about the streets, gracing it with her grand presence?

As for Teague, he went about what had become his usual routine. At the booth of a fruit seller, he purchased some apples. Most of these he took to the booth of one who sold cloth, but some of the apples were given to small children who trailed about behind him. From the seller of cloth, he purchased several yards of fabric which he took to a tailor. From the tailor, he received tunics of various sizes. These he took to the baker. In exchange, the baker gave him a few loaves of fresh-baked bread. These he took to a small house where a little white candle glowed in the window. He knocked quietly and the door opened. Cheerful hello's poured forth into the street, and then the door closed.

Aliatta stood hesitantly outside, uncertain as to how to proceed. After a few moments, the door opened again and a woman stepped out. A smile lit her face as she spotted the girl behind some brush.

"Come in, my child, come in. You must be tired after having walked so far."

Too startled to do otherwise, Aliatta followed the woman into the house, alarmed and slightly ashamed that she had been caught spying.

Once inside, Lady Aliatta looked around at the people who were seated on pillows in what appeared to be a combined dining and visiting area. In addition to the woman who had greeted her at the door, there was an older man whose age was only apparent from his gray hair, a younger couple, two young boys and a little girl. Standing beside them was a young man of average height and build with shaggy brown hair and brown eyes. Her Livid tutor was nowhere in sight.

The young man stepped forward with a smile. "My lady," he said, "I'd like you to meet some old friends of your parents—your real parents. This is Ian and Rosemary, their son Faran and his wife Kamila, and their children Giron, Henry, and Marnie."

"And who ... who are you?" asked Aliatta hesitantly. The speaker's voice was gentle and comforting and he spoke as though he knew her, though she knew for certain they had never met.

The man's eyes widened in revelation and he smiled apologetically as he answered. "I do apologize, my lady. I forgot I had already changed form. That does happen occasionally, the forgetting of which form I am. You know me as your new tutor, Teague Sunray. But in this, my natural form, I am called Levi."

# 12

# IMPOSSIBLE

Not registering. *What? No way. Impossible. Crazy. Lying? Teague? Levi?* Aliatta's head was swirling. Having your mind challenged with new information during a tutoring session is one thing. Having your perception of reality challenged is something else entirely. Teague—or Levi—or whoever he was, spoke again, though Aliatta knew she would be doing well to register anything of what he was saying.

"I am so very sorry to break the news to you in this fashion. I should have listened to the voice that was telling me to remain in Livid form for a bit longer tonight. It is rather exhausting, though, pretending to be someone else for such an extensive period of time."

"Tor ... Torin?" stammered Aliatta from her poor, befuddled brain.

"Oh, he's quite all right," Levi was quick to assure her. "I and a couple of other Livid friends intercepted him on his way home. The other Livids simply persuaded him to take an extended vacation. I connected with his spirit and transformed myself into his likeness—the likeness of what he could be if he were to choose to follow the path of the High King rather than seek the approval and pleasures of the darkness. With those of our people who are now surrounding him—rebuking, challenging, and encouraging him—there is still great hope he may yet begin to attain to what he could become."

The poor girl could only stare blankly at the young man. Nothing made sense at the moment. Her boring Livid tutor had been replaced by his more interesting cousin who was not his cousin but was actually an Adama who was friends with people who had been friends of her parents … That final fact registered.

Her attention swung to the older middle-aged couple. "You knew my parents?"

Ian opened his mouth to reply but was interrupted by the sound of someone pounding heavily upon the door.

"My goodness, this is a busy night," Ian remarked with a wry smile.

"Open up, in the name of the Duke!" called a gruff, cold voice from outside the door.

Nearly all those present gave a wide-eyed gasp of fear. The children drew closer to their parents. Only the grey-haired Ian and the young Levi seemed unaffected. Levi looked to Ian expectantly.

Ian nodded and walked slowly to the door. "I'm coming, sir," he said calmly. "There is no need to break down my door." Then he opened the door to a very frantic Sir Raz.

The man burst into the room. His anger spilled out in a frightening force. "I know she's in here and that tutor too! What has he done with her? I knew he couldn't be trusted and she was foolish enough to try to follow him on her own. It's a wonder she didn't get mobbed! Where are they?"

He stopped short at the sight of one of those for whom he was seeking. She stood in a corner, staring up at him with wide, uncomprehending eyes. At that moment, the proud queen-to-be looked like a lost child, seeking to grasp hold of anything that rang of familiarity. The fight deflated out of him as he stepped forward to guide the young girl back to her castle.

Rosemary's gentle voice stopped him. "There is no need for

alarm, Raz son of Elior," she said. "The girl is quite safe. And now that you are here, we can better proceed in answering her question."

Sir Raz's eyes shot over to Rosemary. Alarm coursed through him as his eyes narrowed in suspicion. "How do you know who I am?"

"As Levi," Rosemary nodded in that person's direction, "already told Aliatta, we are friends of your parents, though I don't believe we ever met. You were already serving and making a name for yourself as a knight at the castle in Zion when we first met your father and mother."

"And Levi is—" questioned Sir Raz, turning to the young man for the first time.

"A servant of the High King and no threat, I assure you," broke in the person of whom they'd been speaking.

Sir Raz nodded absentmindedly and returned his attention to Ian and Rosemary. He looked around the house, walked over to the window to make sure it was well secured, paced, and finally spoke. "I suppose you may as well begin the story then. Things seem to be happening and changing quickly and Aliatta might as well know the full truth about her birth." Sir Raz guided the girl to a nearby pillow, helped her settle in, and then found a place to sit.

Once everyone was comfortably positioned, Rosemary began the narrative. "Aliatta, you were born in the great city of Zion to two wonderful people named Elior and Grace. Your parents loved children but had only been able to have one other child besides you—your brother Raz, born fifteen years prior."

"*This* Raz?" asked Aliatta incredulously, looking over at her weapon's trainer. "Sir Raz the Calculating is my brother?" Their eyes met. Blue eyes looked into a nearly identical set of blue eyes.

Sir Raz nodded solemnly in answer to her question. His voice was abnormally gentle when he spoke and a faraway look filled his eyes. "I still remember the first time I saw you, Little Liat. You had large blue eyes that didn't miss a thing. It was almost as though you were aware of everything going on around you, as though you understood the depths of knowledge, even though you were so new to this world."

They all smiled at the description and then Ian picked up the story in his gruff tone. "Raz left soon after your birth to begin his training. At that time, all the boys in the city and surrounding countryside were being gathered together and put through rigorous exercises. The brightest and strongest were chosen to continue their training with the knights of Zion at the castle. Your brother proved himself again and again, rising quickly through the ranks. In three years, he had earned a position as one of the top guards at the castle. He was privy to a vast amount of secret information and soon learned that the King and Queen were looking for an heir to replace the daughter whom they had loved and lost."

Ian paused and looked to his wife, Rosemary, who continued the story. "About this time, a terrible sickness swept through the city. Being the kind of people they were, your parents shared everything they had and did everything they could to help those who were sick and in need. Your mother always did her best to keep you safe and away from the sickness and death around you, but nobody can keep up that kind of work forever. Your parents were no exception. After a while, they too fell ill.

"They lay in bed, doing their best to help each other. For reasons no one could explain, the sickness didn't get to you. You were as active and energetic as ever, eager to bring food and water to your sickly parents. One night, the food supply ran out, and you left home in search of more. You were wandering the streets when you came upon a house where the aroma of dinner was drifting through an open window. You transformed yourself into a large rat—we still don't know how you were able to do that at so young an age—and entered the house.

"We were all gathered around the table when you came in: Ian, myself, and our two youngest boys who were eleven and thirteen at the time. Suddenly, this giant rat came through the window, jumped onto the table, grabbed hold of some fruit and disappeared out the window again, knocking over our youngest boy in the process. It was all so sudden, we didn't know how to respond. We ran to the window, hoping to follow the large creature, but were stopped short by what we saw. At the edge of the street, the rat turned into a little girl who could have been no more than three years old.

"The Royal carriage was sitting across the street, waiting. The King and Queen must have seen you transform yourself into a rat and decided to intercept you on your way out. With a toss of the Queen's hand one of the carriage guards jumped from his place, picked you up, and handed you over to the King and Queen. We still aren't exactly sure what it was about the act that made them decide then and there to choose you as their heiress. Maybe it was your unconscious connection to the spiritual and what looked to be admirably selfish behavior in their eyes. Maybe they hoped that such a natural affinity for the things of the other realm would prevent you from running away from the Dark One when it was time for you to encounter him—for that is what happened with their daughter. Maybe it was the inner strength displayed in so small a child. Whatever the reason, you were at that moment chosen to be the future Queen of Novus. In order to protect you from experiencing too much of the darkness too soon, they sent you to Earlington to be raised by the Duke and Duchess presiding over the city. Your parents were heartbroken when we finally tracked them down and related all we had seen. Erela of the High King appeared to minister to us and helped us see that it was best to not let your heritage be known. The High King knew where you were and would be continually looking out for you." Rosemary paused and looked knowingly at Raz.

Something clicked for Aliatta. All this time Sir Raz, her brother Raz, had been looking out for her. And even...the High King...cared?

Ian spoke again. "When Raz heard the news, he petitioned to be allowed to serve as your bodyguard and weapons trainer as you grew.

The King and Queen agreed, never realizing that the descendents of those who had once served them were again living and serving in positions of influence. For you see, Aliatta, your great-grandfather was once their Chief Advisor. His daughter was the handmaiden and best friend of the Princess. Her name was—"

"Raziela," Aliatta said softly, putting some more of the pieces together. "Her name is Raziela, right?"

"Yes, but how could you know that?" asked Ian in surprise. "No one has seen or heard from her in many years. The last we heard, she had been imprisoned, probably in Zion, and we all know that no one ever leaves castle dungeons alive."

Aliatta's eyes sparked. "Then it must be her! I met her! She has the most beautiful voice, though she does look rather tired and worn down."

# 13

# GRANDMOTHER

Ian, Rosemary, and Sir Raz looked at one another and broke forth with various exclamations.

"Here in Earlington?"

"Could it be?"

"It must be."

"To think, all this time I've been serving in that castle—"

Sir Raz finally stopped and looked directly at his sister. "Little Liat, that woman is—"

"Our grandmother. I know now. And you must be the descendant she mentioned—the one who will help bring light back to this land!"

Sir Raz caught Rosemary's eye with a questioning look. Rosemary knew what he was thinking and was quick to shake her head in warning before he could answer his sister. *No, do not correct her. She is not ready.*

Sir Raz nodded his agreement. If she was revolted with the idea of being chosen Queen by the physical rulers of this land, how would she react to knowing she had also been chosen by the High King to be Queen? His attention returned to his sister just in time to hear her say—

"Sir Raz, what about our parents?"

"They are still living and serving in Zion," he answered with a thoughtful sigh.

"Can I see them?"

He shook his head regretfully. "I'm afraid that would be far too dangerous."

"But it could be done. I mean … now that I know this—I've heard the truth—you can't expect me to continue living as I always have. How can I go on pretending to be something I'm not?"

"I don't know—" spoke Sir Raz slowly, mentally running a million different scenarios through his mind. "We would have to plan, make the necessary preparations. Even if we had everything in place it would take—"

"The help and guidance of the High King," broke in Levi. He turned to Aliatta. "You will leave, my lady, for that is why I was sent, but it is not yet time. As your brother said, there are preparations which must be made, and until things are in place—until I hear from the High King—you must go on as you always have."

Sir Raz turned to Levi, a cold distrust permeating out from his demeanor. "Who, exactly, are you?"

"My tutor," answered Aliatta pertly.

Sir Raz shook his head, his hard stare never moving away from Levi. His response was spoken as a challenge to the young man. "Your tutor is a Livid, Aliatta."

"Yes," Levi replied.

It took some time, but Levi finally managed to convince the protective brother, knight, and weapon's trainer that they were indeed on the same side. Once mutual trust was finally given—somewhat grudgingly by Sir Raz—they agreed it was time to get Aliatta back to the castle.

An hour later, Aliatta sat at the large dining table with the Duke and Duchess of Earlington as she had done every night for as long as she could remember. Tonight, however, everything felt different. It was as though she were sitting in a foreign world with no idea of how to behave or respond. She fidgeted, pushed her food around on her plate, and gave single syllabic responses to the probing questions of her castle parents. After what—to her—felt like an eternity, Aliatta excused herself to retire for the evening.

The Duke and Duchess watched her go. The moment she exited the room they turned to look at one another, their eyes thick with concern and suspicion.

"Something's going on, Heldric," said the Duchess, her voice heavy with genuine worry. "I don't know what it is, but as a mother, I have a definite feeling that something is different. I know it is!"

Heldric nodded and, rather than disregard her claim of having a "feeling" as he had done on many occasions, he motioned for the servants to snuff out some of the candles. Once the task was completed, he dismissed them.

The room was now silent and dark; the only light came from the two candles which were set before the Duke and Duchess and from four small torches at the corners of the room. Shadows slunk and twisted about on the outskirts of the low lighting.

"Show yourself," commanded the Duke brusquely.

Three forms materialized from the shadows—large, dark masses with a twisted humanoid shape. Perhaps the greatest evidence of their presence was the way they absorbed all traces of the light which was struggling for existence around them.

"Speak," commanded the Duke. "Tell us how things fare in the spiritual realm of this castle and tell us, too, what our little princess has been up to of late."

*There is something different about the atmosphere,* whined one of the creatures. *I occasionally catch small traces of light where before there was only great darkness.*

"A spy?" suggested the Duchess.

"An intruder?" demanded the Duke.

*We don't know!* hissed one of the shadows. *The lights sometimes only flicker briefly and then fade away.*

"How many lights?" the Duke persisted. "Where are these lights?"

The forms twisted as they mumbled various responses of *here and there* and *different places all the time* and *always moving.* Then they paused nervously. Finally one of them spoke up in an uneasy voice. *The lights more often seem to be circulating around the princess.*

"Is this problem something you can handle or must we alert the Master?" asked the Duchess, raising her eyebrow in a threatening manner.

The black forms twisted violently and threw out frantic pleas.

*No, we can handle this ourselves.*

*You know how much trouble we all would be in if he learned we had allowed workers of the Terrifying One into our domain.*

*We will take care of it.*

*He is so busy; there is no need to alert him.*

With a raise of his hand, the Duke brought their panicked entreaties to a halt. "Very well," he said. "We must watch the girl more carefully. We cannot allow her to fall into the hands of the Enemy." With that, he dismissed the Chashaks, though he and the Duchess stayed where they were for quite some time, murmuring and discussing the implications of this new information.

# 14

# WARNING

*L*evi, wake up. A voice spoke urgently, persistently through his subconscious, dreaming mind as the sleeping Livid struggled to return to a state of wakefulness. When he finally did open his eyes, he realized the voice had not been merely in his dreams. A large shimmering figure stood next to his bed.

"That bad is it?" he mumbled aloud.

*I'm afraid so. It is time to move—soon, if not now. They have grown suspicious more quickly than we had hoped. We wait only for the final word of the High King.*

*How much time do you think we have?*

*Less than you need.*

*Do the others know?*

*Baldar and Seok are communicating with them in their dreams right now. I don't think either of them are quite ready to face the full reality.*

*The High King knows though,* Levi said in an attempt to calm his nerves.

*Yes, young servant. He knows.* The Erela focused his brightness more directly upon the young transmogrif. This young, untried servant had been doing well so far, but it was very possible that the trials were about to begin. *Go now to the school room. The Princess is looking for you there.*

\*\*\*

"Oh Teague!" exclaimed Aliatta as soon as he entered the room. "I had the worst dream! There were these awful creatures! They were chasing me and I was running from the castle! And there were these shining things all around us and it was you and me and Sir Raz—but not Raziela! She wasn't with us! We can't leave without my grandmother! I have to go! I have to get her out now!"

"Wait, Aliatta! Calm down! You must calm yourself!" Teague put his hands on her shoulders in an effort to contain in an outward way the inner turmoil that was spilling out of the frightened girl. Inwardly, he thought, *I need to calm down, too.* Then he turned his attention back to the frazzled girl before him. "Calm down, Aliatta," he repeated. His voice was firm, urgent. "You must wait. The High King knows what is happening. He *will* show us a way out. He will also take care of your grandmother. He's brought her this far, hasn't he?"

"Then why wasn't she with me in the dream? It felt so real. It wasn't just a dream, was it?"

Teague shook his head, affirming that it was indeed more than just a dream. Then he continued to speak firmly to her. He must make her listen to him. "Neither was it an actual guarantee of reality. It was a possibility of the future, not a promise of it. We do need to leave—soon. As far as your dream and Raziela is concerned, perhaps there is another way out of the dungeon and Raziela will meet up with us later. I don't know. But I do know the High King—"

"But I *don't* know this High King! How do I know he'll come through?"

"Then trust me!" Teague sought with all his spiritual strength to get Aliatta to look him in the eye, but she steadfastly refused.

"I can't!" She sobbed. Then she shoved herself away and sprinted off down the hallway.

Teague's head dropped down into his branchy hands. He was losing the battle with anxiety and it was now mounting into frustration. What was he supposed to do? Why hadn't he received any further word from the High King?

Continuing in his attempt to fight both the anxiety and the frustration, Teague made his way to the room of Sir Raz. Standing just outside the door, his spirit-spoke to the man inside. *Sir Raz, get up. I know you're awake, I know you had a dream, and I know you don't fully trust me yet, but you need to listen to me. I think your sister is in trouble. She's gone to the dungeon—*

The door flung open and a fully-armed Sir Raz barreled out.

"Where are you going?" cried Teague.

"After her of course!" Sir Raz yelled back.

"But we haven't yet heard—" Teague's voice trailed off as he inwardly finished, *from the High King.* At this point, he wanted to bang his wooden head against a stone wall. How was he supposed to lead a group of people if these two wouldn't even listen to him? Now what was he supposed to do? The last word he had received was to wait, but he had to look after his charges. Teague heaved a great sigh and moved swiftly after Sir Raz, his fear and frustration mounting, halfway contemplating transmogrifying himself into something faster than a Livid.

The Erela who had been attending him called out, *Wait, Levi! Wait! Don't go! Come back!*

For the first time since he had begun his training, Levi was deaf to the call.

The Erela were not the only spiritual beings interested in the movements of the Adamas. Unseen by those agents of light, a skulking dark form had witnessed streaks of light racing by. He quickly and silently summoned several other dark forms. One followed the lights, one went to alert the Duke, and another went to the castle gate where an irritated Livid was stalking toward the towering walls.

Sir Raz finally caught up with Aliatta at the cell of their grandmother, Raziela. The girl was desperately pulling on the bars of the cell. Tears streamed down her face. A large ring of keys lay discarded on the passageway.

"They don't work!" she sobbed hysterically. "None of them work! Why?" She turned and buried her head into Raz while their grandmother murmured soothing words from inside her cell.

A few moments later, Teague arrived breathing heavily, for his Livid body was not accustomed to such swift movements. "We must leave this place," he panted. "Now ..." pant, pant, "We shouldn't be here."

For a while they were all quiet. The magnitude of the situation was fell heavily upon them.

"I'm scared," Aliatta whimpered, her face still buried into her brother's chest.

"What are you scared of Little One?" asked her grandmother gently.

"Of knowing what the dreams meant—of seeing in life what I've seen in my dreams."

Teague nodded sympathetically. "I understand," he said. "But Aliatta, the spirit realm isn't to be feared any more than are the physical things you see. It is simply a part of this life. There are forces of light at work in this world, just as there are forces of darkness. And although the darkness may seem stronger—"

He was interrupted by the sound of heavy footsteps pounding down the dark stone passageway. They scarcely had time to draw breath before a dozen Hellions came into view and surrounded them—sneering, and hissing, eager to attack at any moment. The cavern dungeon seemed darker than ever, as if a thick black fog was swirling around them quenching all sources of light. At a shout from someone in the back, the fearsome guards parted into two lines. Jixgaink Groundcash was the first to appear. He held two large torches and was trembling from head to toe. Following directly behind him was the Duke, the Duchess, and a very smug Torin Spring.

# 15

## THE ESCAPE

Oh my, what have we here?" asked the Duke in a mockingly jovial voice. "A jail break? And twins! Torin, you never told me you had a twin—and an identical twin at that—so identical in fact, that all this time, I thought he was you! Now isn't that funny! Torin, would you do me the honor of introducing me to this brother of yours?"

"He's no brother of mine," droned Torin in all seriousness. His monotone voice carried as much anger and annoyance as it is possible for a monotone to carry. "This *thing* here is an imposter."

The Duke gave a mock gasp of surprise. "You don't say! Well then, I suppose there is only one thing to do." The lighthearted facade disappeared with his next words. "Guards! Throw this lying Livid in the dungeon! Disarm the knight and escort him to his quarters. Make sure he stays there—for now at least. Unfortunately, as it was King Lev who appointed him to his current position, so it is King Lev to whom this dubious knight must answer. As for you," his fiery eyes turned upon Aliatta. "You will be confined to your bedchamber until the Dark One arrives. He will deal with you directly!"

"Father?" Aliatta threw in a desperate plea, hoping—rather than expecting—that it might do some good.

"I'm not your father, Aliatta," replied the Duke in a cold, harsh tone, "a fact of which I suspect you are already well aware."

There was a great deal of hustle and bustle as the guards carried out their duties of securing Aliatta, Raz, and Teague in their assigned locations.

Teague was carelessly tossed into the nearest available cell and then promptly forgotten about.

After that, there was nothing for him to do but to prop himself up as best as he could in his small space and stew over the events which had led to his current situation. His already awkward tree-form made confinement in the musty cell that much more uncomfortable. In a burst of frustration, and convinced it wouldn't make much of a difference anyway, he attempted to transmogrify back into his Adama form. It didn't work. With a cry of anger and frustration, he threw himself against the back wall and groaned. Then, foreseeing no other course of action, he lapsed into a deep brooding silence.

Levi's mind, however, was far from quiet. Anger with himself, annoyance with the circumstances, shame of his failure, desperation for the future, despair for the present—all this and more raced through his mind in a turbulently darkening downward spiral.

Into this darkness, a voice spoke—breaking, or at least interrupting, the accusations and condemnations. "Servant of the High King," whispered a soft but fervent voice, "do not give heed to the enemy's vices. You are so much more than your performance in these events and the High King is greater even than your perceived failures."

"Oh Raziela," he groaned desperately. "What should I do?" Deep inside he knew the source of his tormented thoughts but felt powerless to curtail them.

"The High King desires to speak to you. Simply listen for his voice. Quiet your mind; don't give heed to those other thoughts. Be ready to listen."

Leaning his wooden head back against the cold rock wall, Levi sighed in resignation. *Okay, my King. Well, here I am. I don't know why you chose me for this mission, but I do know you know. Although, with the way I messed things up here tonight, I certainly understand if you want to work with someone else now.*

*Levi, my child,* a firm voice spoke into Levi's spirit. It was not angry, but neither was it a voice to be ignored. *Do you still desire to follow me?*

*Of course, my King, but I don't see what I can do now.*

*Do you still desire to follow me?*

Levi buried his head into branchy hands, still ashamed of his failings, too embarrassed to show his face to the High King. *With all the strength I have left,* he murmured into his hands, all the while wondering how much that was.

*Then follow me now.*

*But tonight, I—*

*There is nothing you can change about what has already happened and you cannot know what the future holds. The present, however, is upon you. What will you do with the present?*

All traces of resistance and excuses left the broken young man and as they did, he discovered a new resolve. *I will serve you, my King.* With these words he lifted his face. The first thing he took note of was that his hands were once again those of an Adama. His eyes traveled up from his hands and settled on a beam of light which was shining down upon him, bathing his human face in warmth, filling him with peace, joy, and a new strength.

*Receive these gifts I give to you. As long as you follow me, they will never leave you. The peace will keep you steady when the situation looks desperate, knowing that I have gone before you and am fighting on your behalf. Joy will give your eyes to see the beauty and goodness beyond the circumstances. My strength, also, I give you. Know that as my servant, I do not ask you to complete these tasks in your own strength, but in the strength I have given you. Now, stand to your feet and look to the left.*

Levi did, regardless of the fact that the command didn't make any sense to him. *I see a light—* Levi's brows furrowed in confusion. *Look closer.*

Levi looked. The light was shining down onto the back left corner of the cell, the corner adjacent to Raziela's cell. It illuminated a special engraving on the stone floor.

*The way out is down and under,* the High King explained.

"Raziela?" Levi asked, now speaking aloud. "Are you seeing what I'm seeing?"

"Indeed I am, young man, and I'm already on it," came a cheerful reply.

The two prisoners knelt on the ground in their respective cells. Following the path of the light, they moved their fingers in intricate patterns around the design. At key points on the engraving, the clank of underground latches could be heard. Finally, their fingers arrived at the center of the design and released the final latch. The engraved tiles sloped downward, revealing a subterranean passageway. Without another word, the prisoners disappeared into the tunnel. At their departure, the ground above them closed back up, immersing them in total darkness. With physical sight now impossible, they held each other's hands and used their spiritual sight to proceed—one step at a time, trusting in the guidance of the High King.

# 16

# BELiEViⲚG

Raz son of Elior paced back and forth across his room. His steps were heavy and his arms were restless. The walls fell victim more than once to an outburst of rage.

While there was certainly plenty to be upset about, most of his anger was directed at himself. He should have listened. He should have known better. All these years—all this time spent pretending to be one of them in order to look after and protect the one he truly cared about—had he somewhere down the line actually turned into one of them? Was he still able to be in the service of the High King or was he more of a liability than an asset? What if he no longer knew how to communicate with the High King? What if he lost his sister forever? Was there even any hope?

His mind went through scenario after scenario—planning, working through possibility after possibility. Finally, he collapsed on his bed in total exhaustion.

*I give up. I have nothing left. I don't know what to do—*

*Well, that's a start,* a voice said.

Sir Raz jumped to his feet and instinctively reached for his sword. His empty scabbard reminded him that he had earlier been disarmed. He surveyed the room, but saw nobody. "Who's there?"

he demanded in a voice which would have made the blood of his enemies run cold. "Where are you?"

The voice answered calmly, completely unaffected by Sir Raz's threatening tone. *I am the One whom you are seeking. I have never left. You have been given much and have learned to work and thrive in matters regarding the kingdom of the Dark One. Now it is time for you to learn how to operate in my kingdom. The skills you have learned will help you—later. But first, you must learn how to operate in a different fashion. Close your eyes. Do not rely on your physical sight. Look around and tell me what you see.*

Scarcely aware of what he was doing, Sir Raz did as he was instructed. A single shimmering figure loomed large and imposing before the door. There was something startlingly familiar about it. A childhood memory rose up and he knew then what it was.

"I see one of your messengers," he said.

*Yes. He will speak for me and be your guide. Listen to him and obey. And though he will now be the voice you hear, I will always be watching and directing.*

"Are there none of the other kind in this room?" he asked.

*Not at this time. They do not yet know what you are and so they think you are harmless. Therefore, they have stationed and occupied themselves elsewhere.*

"Aliatta!" His eyes flew open in alarm as he became instantly aware of just where that 'elsewhere' was. Much to his surprise, he could still see the sparkling presence.

The messenger nodded. His sister was indeed experiencing the presence of "the other kind."

Sir Raz bounded for the door, but the Erela blocked his path and shook his head. With a resigned sigh, Raz reluctantly plopped back down upon the bed.

*You have long relied on your own strength*, it said. *Now it is time for you to learn how to trust and rely on the High King. Your sister has a decision to make. The decision must be hers and the action must*

*come from her alone, but do not worry, for she will have help. Gather*
*everything you need for the four of you to take on a long journey, but*
*wait here. If all goes well, your sister will come to you.*

"And if it doesn't?"

*Then we will wait for further instructions from the High King and*
*do as he directs.*

Sir Raz was not exactly satisfied with this answer, but he realized
that if he wanted to serve the High King, there was nothing else to
be done but to follow the instructions and wait. But he didn't have
to wait and do nothing. The Erela had given him another task. Sir
Raz jumped out of bed, removed his bedsheet, and began setting
everything he perceived they would need on it. His final act was to
strap on all the stashed weapons he kept carefully hidden. Then he
sat on the bed and waited. And while he waited, he wondered how
his sister was doing.

Unfortunately, his sister wasn't doing much better than he or
Levi had been doing at the beginning. She was, at the moment,
lying on her bed sobbing, too distraught to think about anything.
Everything felt hopeless. Despair lay heavily upon her.

Gradually, exhaustion—and something else—came over her,
and her frenzied tears stopped. She felt a sudden warmth and
peace—a feeling that was somewhat familiar. She lay still with her
eyes closed for several minutes—savoring the comfort which enveloped her like a warm, cozy blanket.

When she finally opened her eyes, she was startled to see a man
standing before her bed. He was covered in the smoothest amour
she had ever seen, marked with a signet she didn't recognize. A long
red cloak fell from the center of his back. His skin and clothing
seemed to glow, though not in an overwhelming manner. Strange as
it seemed, there was again, something familiar about the situation.
In a flash, Aliatta remembered her dream from over a month ago.

"Who are you?" she asked, as one who is awakening from a dream. "Am I dreaming?"

*My name is Melhem*, it answered. *I am a messenger of light in the service of the High King. I am an Erela, and no, you are not dreaming. But you have seen me in your dreams before, though I was shown to you there in my full brilliance and have now lessened the effect so as not to unduly alarm you.*

"But if you were in my dreams, and you're here now, then that other creature—"

*Is also real.*

"What is it? Where did it come from? Is it here, too?" Worry and fear began to creep again into the heart and mind of the girl.

*It was once an Erela like myself—a strong, beautiful creature of light, created by the High King at the beginning of the world. Out from the heart of the High King, His hands, His words, He gathered the light of the stars, mixing it with His own indescribable brightness. Wisdom poured forth as He fashioned the light into beautiful, crystalline beings—the Erela. We were made to be the reflection of His own brilliance and goodness. One of us was made to stand supreme above all the rest. He was stronger, more beautiful, more brilliant—the epitome of splendor and radiance. He was appointed Chief Commander of the Erela. His heart, however, was not long with the High King. You see, he had hopes from the beginning of being made king over the land of Novus. When he discovered the High King had appointed the Adamas to that position, he was infuriated. Jealousy, arrogance, and anger raged through him, and it wasn't long before the form which was meant to radiate light, radiated darkness instead. Through smooth, deceptive, persuasive words, he convinced many of the other Erela to join him. As each one turned against the will and purpose of the High King, they too became darkened and their once beautiful forms became twisted and warped. These darkened Erela are now known as Chashaks. They have placed themselves under the charge of their commander—the Dark One—and seek nothing less than to keep the Adamas and all others in creation from serving the High King. In the same way their own forms were distorted and weakened, they seek also to prevent all others from becoming the beautiful and powerful creatures they were meant to be.*

"Are these Chashaks … are they strong?"

*They have as much power as they are given by the physical beings of this world, but in general, they are continually trying to be something other than what they were made to be and that itself weakens them.*

"Tell me how I can fight them! I know how to fight. I'm not afraid!" Aliatta's previous feeling of fear towards these creatures had momentarily left her memory so that she was now convinced of her own superiority and ability to defeat such unworthy opponents. Her puffed up arrogance, however, was quickly deflated by Melhem's next words.

*You cannot fight them, at least not successfully or directly, and certainly not in your own strength. The High King will protect you and fight for you, for it is His strength and authority that can save you. The way you can fight is by standing firm—by choosing the light and the truth over the darkness and by placing your trust in the High King.*

There was silence as Aliatta took some time to absorb and process this new information. It went against everything she had learned in weapons training. But then again, those weapons were for physical beings. This brought another thought to the forefront of her mind. "Melhem, why have I never seen the Erelas or Chashaks before?"

*After the Dark One's deception of King Lev and Queen Malka, the High King placed a barrier between the physical and spiritual world—a barrier which had never been there before. He placed a veil over the spiritual eyes of those on earth, causing the spiritual to become invisible and intangible for the purpose of lessening the influence the Dark One might be able to have. Now, only those who seek the spiritual can see it, for better or for worse. Although the Dark One has certainly found many other ways to cause chaos and pain, he is no longer able to cause physical harm with his spiritual body. He is no longer able to deceive people with his beautiful and powerful appearance.*

"I can see you. Will I now be able to see these servants of the Dark One?" Aliatta felt her previous proclamation of bravado sliding away at the prospect of actually seeing these creatures.

Throughout all of Aliatta's fluctuating emotions, the calm clear voice of the Erela had remained unchanged. *For one purpose you will now see them—so that you may be fully aware of the choice which is before you. The High King is in need of someone to complete a very specific task. It is a task which you will be able to do. The choice is yours. Will you take on the position from the High King, or will you take the path on which the Dark One would have you go? There is no middle ground.*

The girl's eyes furrowed in doubt. "What about Elsie, the lost Princess of Novus?" she asked. "I thought she serves neither the High King nor the Dark One."

*Although she likes to believe that, and the Dark One allows her to think she serves no one, it is not true, for in serving herself, Elsie does indeed serve the purposes of the Dark One. Now, are you ready to see the paths before you?*

Aliatta was silent and the Erela said no more as she sat contemplating her choice. Finally, she gave a timid nod. In contrast to the timidity of the nod, her eyes blazed with decision.

# 17

## CHOICE

At first there was only a faint dimming or sharpening of the colors around her. There were places where the colors brightened—becoming more clear and vivid than ever before. Then there were other places where the colors took on a sickly-looking shade. Aliatta focused in on these areas of color change and soon began to see vague outlines emerging. After a while, the outlines of distinct forms were visible. The outlines filled in, revealing the full essence of two distinct types of spiritual beings. One form was large and strong and stood upright, calm, confident. This kind exuded an air of peaceful waiting. There were only two of them—one other besides Melhem (who had returned to his full brilliance). Together they shone forth a light which made everything it touched appear brighter and more vibrant than ever before.

*The full essence of an Erela*, thought Aliatta. Her body shook in breathless awe as she gazed upon them.

Then she turned reluctantly but curiously to look at the others. As she did, she let forth an involuntary gasp of dismay. Though not as terrifying as the creature in her dream, these forms were also large and imposing. Their figures, however, were not upright, but were hunched and crumpled, as though someone had taken a beautiful statue when the clay was still soft and had scrunched it down so that the features were bent and distorted. There was an anxious, desperate vibration radiating through them (there were at least half a dozen present). Some sneered and reached out hands with sharpened nails. Others twitched anxiously, causing her to involuntarily twitch and tense up in response. One of them whined pitifully.

She didn't need to be told that these pathetic and menacing creatures were the Chashaks.

One of them began to speak. *Don't listen to those bright ones*, it whined. *They will only lead you to peril and death. Much better to look out for yourself and take the path which will lead to the least amount of trouble.*

*Yes*, chimed in another. *You don't want to cause more trouble for yourself and your friends. Just stay as you are and things will work themselves out.*

*You could rule over all Novus*, coaxed one in a sickly sweet voice.

*And if you go, you will die!* threatened the one who seemed to be the leader. He made a menacing move towards her, reaching out his hand as though to secure his claim.

Into the commotion and confusion, another voice spoke clear, strong and with authority. *Enough!* It thundered through the room piercing the hearts of those present. The Chashaks silenced instantly and cowered in trembling fear, for the voice had not come from the Erela, who continued to stand unmoved. This same powerful voice, in a more loving and cherishing tone, then spoke to Aliatta. *The time has come to make a choice. You must either look towards my messengers the Erela and decide to follow me in the ways I will show you, or set your eyes upon the darkness and follow them in the ways of the Dark One.*

"Will I be safe with you?" she asked hesitantly.

*There will be dangers, but as long as you seek after my ways, I will fight your battles.*

The girl nodded. The cacophony of Chashak noises began again and quickly escalated to a deafening din. Resolutely, though not without fear, Aliatta—the heir to the throne of Novus, the grand-daughter of the Writer, one chosen by the High King—turned her eyes to the Erela. She focused on the light and peace which was being reflected out through their being. Then she got up from her bed and took a step in their direction. The clamor of the Chashaks faded slightly. She took another step, never removing her gaze from the Erela who stood before her. The dark noise lessened even more. With each step, she became more and more deaf to the darkness and her senses awakened more and more to the light.

Behind her, the Chashaks roared and raged. They advanced upon her and reached out to take hold of her in an effort to force her to the path of the Dark One. Their claws, however, found no hold and moved harmlessly through her.

Aliatta arrived at the locked door and grasped hold of the handle. It swung open without protest and she stepped into the hall, her eyes still fixed upon the two shimmering beings. As they walked down the hall, three more Erela appeared and stationed themselves around her. Though she looked neither to the right nor the left and saw nothing other than what was directly in front of her, Aliatta somehow knew without a doubt exactly where they were going.

Behind her, the Chashaks sprang into action. Immediately upon discovering that they held no power over her, they dispersed to seek help from those they were able to influence. Two went to alert the Duke and Duchess, others went to alert the guards and anyone else in the castle who might understand the gravity of the situation, and one unlucky Chashak fearfully made his way to inform the Dark One himself of their failure to contain, confine, and control the one whom they had intended to be the Queen of darkness. While this latter unfortunate figure wondered and worried about how the Dark One would respond once he received this news, the other Chashaks were facing their own frustrations. They had succeeded in waking the castle. Regrettably for them, most of those they had awakened were not sufficiently attuned to the spiritual to be able to understand what the Chashaks were trying to communicate. This resulted in a whole bunch of people running wildly about without knowing exactly what it was they were chasing.

The moment Aliatta arrived at Sir Raz's chambers, the door opened and her brother stepped out with a gathered-together, packed-full bedsheet hoisted over his shoulders. Chaos raged all around; creatures bustled here and there, their eyes and mannerisms suggesting that they were frantically searching for something. When the castle guards came upon Sir Raz and Aliatta, they moved conveniently out of the way, their unchanged manner suggesting they were unaware of what they had done. In this way, Sir Raz and Aliatta, in keeping their eyes fully trained on the Erela, were able to flawlessly navigate through the swarm of people who were searching for what was right under their very noses. The escapees soon turned off the main hallway, passed through a scarcely visible side door, and found themselves maneuvering through little-used servants' passageways. Before they knew it, the Erela were leading them through another side door. This door led outside and happened to be where all the castle garbage was tossed to be burned. The Erela carefully directed them through the compost to the far side.

Here they stopped. Sir Raz fumbled through his make-shift bag and produced a set of boy's clothing. These he handed to Aliatta, along with a gray cloak which would serve as her travel disguise. Once she made the change, Raz carefully placed her royal dress into the bag.

"You never know when we might need it," he explained.

Sir Raz and Aliatta made their way north through the city to the thick forests beyond, continuing to follow the shimmering messengers of the High King.

As they approached the woods, Sir Raz caught sight of another group to the east who was cautiously making their way towards them. By force of habit, he thrust Aliatta behind him and drew his sword.

*Peace, my children.*

Sir Raz and Aliatta simultaneously heard the calm, beautiful voice echoing through their minds. They gasped in unbelief when they realized the voice belonged to their grandmother, Raziela. Levi walked alongside her and behind them was a group of other Adamas from the city.

The Erela beckoned the refugees onward and into the forest where there was greater cover. Once these messengers received notice that it was safe, the caravan stopped and the unspoken covering of silence was lifted. Hugs were exchanged, introductions were made, and explanations were rapidly given:

The tunnel Raziela and Levi followed had come up in the middle of Ian's kitchen, giving the family quite a fright.

After being quickly appraised of the situation, Ian had gone about the business of gathering others in the city who were also of the light. A few had chosen to accompany him and his family from the city while others had felt the need to stay and shine a light in Earlington for those who might benefit from it.

Aliatta found herself struggling to pay attention, though she did manage to make the appropriate responses when needed. Her mind, however, was drifting to the north.

It was Levi who, noticing the yawns and sleep-filled eyes of the children, suggested they find a place to bed down for a few hours of sleep.

They followed the Erela to a hidden cave, spread out the blankets Sir Raz and Rosemary had brought, and laid down.

As he began to drift off into a welcome sleep, Sir Raz heard a clear voice beside him say, "How far is it to Zion from here?"

In a sleep-fogged frame of mind, he gave his sister a confused look and then answered her in the tone that people may occasionally use on young children when they just want them to stop talking. "About 150 miles as the eagle flies. Why?"

"I want to go get mother and father and bring them with us." Her voice, unlike her brother's, held no trace of grogginess.

Sir Raz immediately dismissed the idea as impractical and, in his exhausted state, assumed Aliatta would realize the impossibility of it as well. Therefore, he answered her with a "Good one, Aliatta. Very funny," and returned promptly to sleep.

When he awoke the next morning, she was gone.

# 18

# THE CHANGE IN PLANS

So what do we do now?"

The eleven Adamas who had accompanied Ian and Rosemary in their exodus from the city had huddled up to discuss this new situation. They weren't entirely sure who it was they should look to for leadership: Sir Raz—the trained fighter, Levi—the transmogrif who had journeyed from the camp of the Loyal Ones, Raziela—the Writer and one who had been a part of life on Novus from the beginning, or Ian and Rosemary—the elders whom they had followed from Earlington.

In case you are wondering who these other people are, I will take a moment to tell you just a little about them. First, there is Faran and his wife Kamila. Faran is Ian and Rosemary's son. He and Kamila have three children—two boys and a little girl. Giron is ten, Henry is eight, and little Marnie is six. Then there is Reut and Maya—twins in their late teenage years who have been taking care of each other since their parents died less than a year ago. The final family consists of Benicio and Livna with their young teenage sons, Sean and Zavier. Benicio and Livna had heard whispers of a settlement to the south where the Loyal Ones lived in peace and they felt it was time for them to go there. Sean and Zavier are of course looking forward to some adventures and are hoping for the opportunity to take part in some fighting down the road. We shall see whether or not this latter hope is realized.

While the above-mentioned people had been jabbering and worrying amongst themselves, Sir Raz had been sitting dejectedly in a corner, berating himself for yet another failure (or perceived failure anyway); Levi had been having a silent conversation with the Erelas; Raziela had been listening and trying to connect spiritually to wherever Aliatta was; and Ian and Rosemary had been engaged in a private conversation with each other while they sat sketching something in the dirt of the cave.

Finally, Levi spoke up in a calm, matter-of-fact manner. "The purpose of this journey," he said, "had originally been for all of us to go south together to the settlement of the Loyal Ones. Aliatta's departure has obviously altered that plan, but has not entirely disrupted it. There is for Aliatta an unexpected benefit in the direction she has chosen to go—" He paused and looked expectantly to Sir Raz.

It took Sir Raz a moment to pick up on what Levi was alluding to—after all, his confidence was still shaky after having lost his little sister twice in a single day. Then, it clicked. "The strategic benefit," he said slowly, "is that the Dark One will have left Zion by now and no one would even think to look for her north of Earlington."

Levi nodded, casting an encouraging smile in the direction of Sir Raz. Then he continued speaking. "Aliatta has acted on her own, without consulting or trusting to the counsel of the High King or anyone else. I have been speaking to the High King on her behalf, and though she acted foolishly, her desire for her parents was at least a pure-hearted one—one that the High King will honor. The altered plan then is this: we will split up, at least for the time being. The rest of you will journey south as planned and—"

"I will go after my sister," interjected Sir Raz, rising to his feet.

Though Levi's heart was sympathetic toward the man, his voice was firm. "No, Sir Raz. You will travel with the others. This group will need the skills you possess—skills that I do not have. They will need the protection and training you can provide, as well as the quick analytic assessment you can give of the situations. Raziela will help you hear and understand the directions from the High King. Ian and Rosemary know where to find the safe contacts you'll need for the journey. I will go after Aliatta and, under the guidance and protection of the High King, bring both her and your parents safely out of Zion. We will then do our best to meet up with you in the village south of Redford Palace."

Sir Raz was obviously less than pleased by this arrangement, but after an inward battle, his analytical mind kicked in and he realized it was indeed the best option. "It would be safer for us to lay low here for a few days," he said. "—give the Dark One and his forces the chance to search out the areas to south."

Levi nodded in agreement, relieved to see Raz regaining his confidence. Then he turned to Raziela. "Were you able to get a read on where Aliatta is?" he asked.

Raziela nodded and the two of them stepped aside to discuss her whereabouts. Shortly after, Levi gathered a couple of bread rolls from the food supply, checked to make sure his water skin was filled, collected Aliatta's water skin from Raz, said his goodbye's, and left.

"He's going alone?" asked the teenager, Zavier. The question came not out of fear for Levi's safety but rather from regret that he had not been invited to go along.

"He's never alone," said Raziela with a cheerful smile, fully comprehending the young man's real concern. "But since we are going to be here for a few days, what do you say to a few lessons in fighting and swordplay, given by our very own Sir Raz the Calculating."

Giron and Henry cheered audibly while the other teenagers merely grinned (they were much too dignified to cheer like such little children).

Sir Raz cast his grandmother a shocked 'are-you-serious' look.

Raziela grinned. He shook his head at her antics, shrugged, then moved to begin the lessons. *Probably for the best*, he thought. *The more fighters we have in the group, the better.*

Unseen by most of the others, the Erela, Baldar, was standing guard at the cave entrance. He watched Levi depart with a vigilant eye. Another Erela, Seok, stood amongst the group, reflecting onto them the peace and calm of the High King. Melhem had departed earlier with Aliatta, for the High King does not wait to be asked before he offers his protection.

Soon after leaving the cave, Levi transmogrified into a wolf for better speed and tracking capability. With those helpful traits, along with the information Raziela had given him as to the approximate location of Aliatta, it wasn't long before he found the girl. She had already made it several miles through the forest and had just sat down next to a tree to rest when he came upon her.

Careful not to make any alarming noises, Levi changed back into his Adama form and nonchalantly walked into view.

"That's a long walk you've had," he mentioned casually. "And you don't even have any food or water to help your body recuperate."

Aliatta's head shot up in surprise. She was too shocked to say anything in response.

Levi sauntered over to where she was sitting, passed her a roll and her water skin, and sat down next to her on the forest floor.

Aliatta took the offerings with a mumbled thank you, her eyes cast downward and an embarrassed flush filling her cheeks. Up until that moment she hadn't felt any shame or remorse for the actions she had taken.

They ate in silence. Levi seemed content to wait for Aliatta to speak. Finally, she did.

"I should have told somebody," she said quietly, still looking down.

"That would have been helpful," Levi agreed.

"Did I cause a lot of worry?" She looked up at him now, her brows furrowed in concern.

Levi nodded.

"I didn't think to ask or talk to anybody about this."

"And you didn't think to talk to the High King about it, either," Levi added.

Her eyes widened in alarm. "Do you think He is upset with me?"

Levi shook his head. "The High King doesn't get upset or angry in the way we do with each other. Would He rather have had you confer with Him? Of course, but for your own good. He knows your heart, Aliatta. He knows your desire to see your parents. And He knows that you are just beginning to learn how to walk with Him. Your mistakes do not make Him angry or upset. Oh, Aliatta, you didn't even think to bring any food and water with you. Do you even know how to get to Zion?"

"Not ... exactly ..."

"We should have studied geography," Levi said wryly. "And you are planning to travel on foot? That is going to take a while. In fact, it may take long enough for the Dark One to return to Zion. No, he isn't there now. He has gone to Earlington to search for you and will undoubtedly search the areas to the south before he searches north. We at least have that to our advantage."

"We?" asked Aliatta with a hint of hope.

"You don't think I came all the way out here just to lecture you? Though you did not ask him, the High King has approved your quest. He sent me to help you and will himself be looking out for us. Now, time for a lesson in Novus geography."

"Lessons? Now?"

"Of course. What better time to learn geography than when you are about to travel across it?" Levi cleared away some of the forest brush to reveal a smooth, dirt writing board. Then he picked up a stick and started to draw. "This is Earlington and this is where we are, in Crels Forest. It isn't the largest forest in Novus, but it is certainly big enough. It stretches north for about 50 miles before running into the Teman River. This section of the Teman is only about … 10 miles wide, but over here, to the east, it widens to at least 25 miles. Once we cross the Teman, we'll be on a flat section of land known as Merchant's Haven. The Qatan Forest covers most of this area, but the merchants have cleared enough trees to build themselves the settlement of Stratham. To the east of Merchant's Haven is the ten-mile wide Maarab River and across that river, is Zion's Island. Seventy-five miles up the coast, in order to better trade with Zion, the merchants built a bridge across the river—quite an amazing feat, really. That bridge is how we will get to the city."

"That's a long way," Aliatta grunted.

Levi nodded.

"How did you get here so fast?" she asked suddenly. "It took me all night to get this far. When did you leave?"

"Sometime this morning."

"Then, how—"

Levi smiled. "Would you like to find out? If we are going to get to Zion in a timely and unsuspecting manner, we will need to travel faster than our Adama legs will take us."

# 19

# Transmogrification

Thus began the lessons on transmogrifying—changing themselves into other animals. Before each transformation, Levi would instruct her as to the nature of the creature—the strengths and weaknesses and the standard creature behavior.

"The wolf, Aliatta," he would say, "is a long distance endurance runner. He can run up to 125 miles in a day. Since he never knows when his next meal will be, he'll often eat up to a fifth of his body weight to make up for the days when he can't find food. He is fearsome, so he's left alone by most of the other animals—"

He would also instruct her as to the spiritual nature of transmogrification. "You first need to be connected to the Spirit of the High King. With this connection in place, you can then turn your attention to the creature whose likeness you want to take on. In this way, you become a creature whose spirit is ultimately connected to the High King—a creature as it was meant to be under the guidance and direction of the ultimate Life Giver. But it is very important you never forget who you truly are or desire to leave behind forever the Adama form the High King gave you—for if that happens, you can never return to your original state. You would, in fact, begin to lose what it is that makes you human. To return to your Adama state, you must think on who it is that the High King made you to be. These changes we are making are temporary. They are meant to serve for a time and not to transform us forever into something other than that which we were created to be."

And so their days on the trail passed by. A short breakfast would be followed by a tutorial on a couple of specific creatures. Following this tutorial, Levi would transform into that creature and then guide Aliatta in the transmogrification process. The first couple of lessons were mainly for practice in order to get Aliatta accustomed to changing into something else and then back again. She would need to be fairly proficient at this by the time they reached Zion if she were going to make use of the skill while they searched for her parents.

At first, the changes took a long time for Aliatta to complete. She was still learning to connect to the spiritual and you may imagine she felt some trepidation at the idea of fully transforming into something else, for there was also the unspoken concern that she may not be able to change back. It was, in fact, the changing back part which proved to be the most difficult. Aliatta, like many twelve-year-olds, had not yet acquired a clear picture of who she was. Therefore, when it came time to return to Adama form, Levi would remind Aliatta of who she was and allow her to lean on his confidence until such a time as she could take full ownership of her own identity.

At some point during the day or night (depending upon the nature of the creature they were at the time), they would travel. Levi used these times to instruct Aliatta on more aspects of the High King.

"Do you see those stars up there, Aliatta?" he said one night as they flew across the sky. "There are countless numbers of them, and yet the High King knows each and every one of them. Do you realize that you are more beautiful and precious to him than those stars?"

Another day, as they were walking through the forest, he brought her attention to the multi-colored flowers interspersed among the brush and trees. "Look at the flowers we are walking by," he said.

"Few creatures are even aware of their existence here. No one comes to take care of them, and yet they grow, for the High King himself cares for them. He dresses them beautifully, each one a unique creation. Are we not more precious to him than these flowers?"

In this way, after a few days' time (a fraction of the time it would have taken them to travel in their Adama form), they had traversed the Crels Forest, crossed the Teman River to the north, passed through the Qatan forest (bypassing Stratham), and arrived at the bridge which would take them across the Maarab River to the gates of Zion.

The days of travel had been pleasant, albeit more than a little exhausting, and Aliatta found herself lamenting that this part of the journey was now at an end. There had been freedom and a daily challenge. But from this point on, they would have to use caution. More than one life would be endangered by their presence and it was almost certain that their travels hereafter would not be nearly as leisurely.

After a bit of discussion, and more than a few conversations with the High King, it was decided they would take the form of rats and cross the bridge in a merchant's cart. They began to keep a close eye on each of the merchants who daily made their way back and forth across the bridge. Levi wasn't really comfortable with any of them, but at last chose a cart driven by someone who didn't feel quite as dark as the other merchants. In their rodent form, they neatly hopped aboard the produce-laden cart and enjoyed an easy ride across the bridge, up the hill, and into the city.

The hustle and bustle of Zion nearly overwhelmed Aliatta. The streets were crowded and dirty. People were either arguing and yelling at each other or were already engaged in settling their disagreements with full-out fights. Small children ran through the streets, either begging for money or expertly relieving people of their monetary possessions. There was certainly no shortage of rats.

Levi also found himself shocked by the environment of Zion,

though from a different perspective. It was spiritually dark—far darker than any place he had ever been. The air itself felt heavy and suffocating. The pain, anger, hatred, lust, greed, frivolity, hopelessness, depression of a thousand spirits assaulted him to such a degree that for a few moments he was unable to maintain a clear connection with the High King. And then he saw it. A shining beacon in the center of the city lit up the sky and gave him hope once more. He heard the High King say, *That is the place you seek.*

*Come on Aliatta*, he spirit-spoke to her. *I know where your parents are.*

It took him a couple of minutes to get her attention, for she was still stunned by the chaos and conditions she saw all around her. However, by nudging her and chattering to her as much as he could in rat form, Aliatta finally acknowledge him.

*I never thought it would be so bad here. Or did I somehow know? Is this why I never wanted to come?* she asked.

*I think you sensed it, though you couldn't put words to it. I also think that something in you has maintained a connection to your parents, and through them, to this city. Speaking of your parents, Aliatta, I know where they are.*

A pair of rat eyes widened and brightened. *How do you know?*

*They're the only light I can see in this place and they shine rather brightly for those who have eyes to see. Watch me carefully now. Getting to them may be a bit tricky in this form.*

*I think it would be tricky in any form,* said Aliatta wryly.

Levi paid careful attention to where their cart was going, always keeping his spirit focused on the shining lighthouse in the middle of the city. Before long, he and Aliatta jumped off the cart and scurried off on a hectic scramble through the bustling city streets, watching out for busy feet, jumping over random objects, and keeping an eye out for predators. Being in rat form certainly had its advantages, but it also came with its share of disadvantages, like having to watch out for cats who wouldn't think twice about eating you.

After what seemed like forever, they arrived at a little wooden house where a white candle shone cheerily in the window. As Aliatta stared at the house, she started to feel very nervous and soon discovered she could barely move. What if they didn't like her? What if they told her to go back or that it was better for her to become Queen of Novus and they turned her over to the King and Queen. What if—?

Levi tried to prompt Aliatta-rat forward. After several unsuccessful attempts, he changed his tactic and went directly to the door. As soon as he arrived, the door opened.

A woman stepped out, causing Levi to do a double-take, for in many ways, she was a mirror image of Aliatta. A few lines on her face gave evidence to hardships overcome. Her eyes were hazel compared to Aliatta's eyes of blue, and her hair was light brown rather than Aliatta's dark black tresses, but her height, stature, and general coloring were definitely those of Aliatta.

The hazel eyes had been bright and expectant when the woman first looked out, but they turned to confusion as she spotted one rat directly in front of the door, and a smaller one shivering at its edge. She stood listening for a time, then shrugged.

"Come in, little friend," she said softly to Levi. "And you too," she spoke to Aliatta-rat. "It's ok. I'm not going to hurt you." When the littlest rat didn't budge, the woman walked over and gently picked her up. Then she took both rats into her home.

# 20

# THE PURSUIT

O nce inside, the woman set the two rats softly on the floor. Then she knelt down beside them and just sat there, studying them.

After a few minutes, she spoke. Her voice was soft, hesitant, and carried an interesting blend of confusion and amusement. "Well," she said, almost to herself. "This certainly isn't what I'd expected when I opened the door. But I know I heard the High King correctly. He told me to be ready and then to go to the door because the one I had been longing for had returned. But, maybe you two little creatures are to take me to her?" She gazed at them very intensely—searching for a sign. Finding nothing, she leaned back with a sigh. "Or maybe I'm going crazy talking to a couple of rats. What do you think?"

The two rodents had not moved from the place she had set them. The timid rat was still shivering nervously. The other one, however, seemed to be trying to communicate something to the fearful rat by using a series of squeaks and nudges. Finally, it gave up, scurried over to where she sat, and looked her full in the face.

*The message was not wrong, as you will soon see,* she heard a voice say. *But first, I'm going to do something which may startle you. In fact,*

*both rats will undergo a similar change. Please try not to be too alarmed.*
*We are not who we seem to be.*

She nodded to show she had received the message, wherever it had come from, then gasped in surprise as the rat who'd crawled up to her started to change form. He stretched and grew and as he grew, the coarse dark hair of the rodent was replaced by a sturdy set of animal-hide clothing. When the transformation (which happened in a matter of seconds) was complete, a young man stood in the place where a rat had just been.

"Excuse me for a minute, Ma'am," were his first hurried and absentminded words to her in this Adama form.

"Grace, I'm Grace," she found herself saying in a rather muddled frame of mind. She had heard tales of these shape changers, but had never in her life actually met one or been a witness to the transmogrification process.

He met her eyes and nodded to acknowledge the request. "Excuse me for a moment, Grace," he repeated, this time in a softer and more polite manner. "I promise I'll give you more explanations soon." He turned to the other rat and began making a series of squeaks, sometimes stroking it as though to give it some reassurance. Finally, the rat gave him a squeak in response and he stepped back.

The woman watched as the transformation she had just seen was repeated in a similar fashion. This change, however, took longer and even contained periods where it appeared nothing was happening (this was a rather awkward stage to behold, as during these pauses there would be a combination of rat and human features). In these moments, the young man would offer words of encouragement and the transformation would continue.

Finally, the change was complete. Before Grace, there now stood a beautiful young girl with long black hair and clear blue eyes. Her mother's heart immediately knew who it was she was gazing upon. With tears in her eyes, she stepped forward and wrapped the girl in a full mother's hug. Years of yearning, of wishing, of missed embraces all flooded out of her. She knew it might be awkward for the girl—as indeed it was at first—but Grace was powerless to stop the torrent.

Aliatta responded stiffly at first, as though the she wasn't sure what to do or how to respond, but that discomfort gradually faded as she allowed herself to relax into the arms of her mother. *So this is what a real mother's love feels like*, thought Aliatta as she reveled in a peace she had never before known.

When they stepped back, tears were streaming down their faces and even Levi found himself brushing away a tear or two.

It was in this state that Elior son of Meir found them. You may imagine the surprise he felt when he beheld the scene before him. He was just returning from his shop in the marketplace where he crafted and sold items of wood, as well as the fine clothing that Grace tailored. His head was full of the happenings of the day and he was in the middle of reflecting upon the argumentative customer with whom he had barely managed to avoid coming to blows. How he had longed for the peace and quiet of their home ... So imagine, if you will, his surprise at entering his home and discovering not only his wife, but two others whom he did not know—all huddled together—chatting and laughing with tears running down their cheeks. What is a poor, exhausted, caught-off-guard man to do?

As it was, he didn't do much for the first few minutes. He somehow had enough presence of mind to be sure that the house was secured—all windows covered and the door locked. Then he looked from his wife to the girl ... then back to his wife ... then to the girl ... then understanding dawned. His eyes widened and his voice was choked up as he turned to his wife and stammered, "Is this ... is this—"

Grace nodded.

Before Aliatta had a chance to say anything, she found herself wrapped in a huge bear hug by a tall, broad shouldered man. He buried his face in her hair as he mumbled, "It's her—my little girl.

My little girl has returned—" Sobs shook his large frame as Grace stood by, lending him what peace she could.

As for Aliatta, she again fought through the initial awkwardness, and then, as she allowed herself to melt into her father's embrace, realized she had never before felt so much safety and comfort. *Is this anything like the love Levi says the High King has for me,* she wondered. *Is this how it would feel to be fully wrapped in His protection?*

The hugs and greetings, with their emotional deluge, finally ran their course, leaving each member present feeling quite drained. Grace tore herself away from the gathering long enough to set dinner out, and while they ate, Levi and Aliatta shared their stories and adventures.

Long after Aliatta had gone to sleep for the night, Elior, Grace, and Levi stayed up talking. There was much to discuss. Of primary importance was how to get them all out of the city.

"Although the King and Queen do not know of our connection to their family through Raziela and Aliatta," said Elior, "we have been noticed and singled out for other reasons. Grace makes beautiful clothing and her services are in great demand by Queen Malka. My carpentry skills have also come to their attention. In fact, we will be going to the castle tomorrow to deliver our latest products. This favor has allowed us to move freely within the city and even to the forest beyond where I find the lumber I need for my work and Grace finds the dyes she needs for hers. However, I fear this attention will also make it more difficult for us to leave the city for an extended time without being noticed. Written permission must be applied for and given to all who come and go from Zion."

Their conversation continued well into the night, though they were careful to extinguish the candle at the regular time so as not to arouse suspicions.

The next morning, Elior and Grace made their way to the castle. The Queen, as always, was enthralled by Grace's bright and tasteful creations. The King was appropriately pleased, though less vocal than his wife, about the new bow Elior presented to him. Once the items were received and paid for, Elior handed the King his request to leave the city. "I am in need of more wood, and my wife must herself seek the special flower which allows her to make such beautiful clothing for her majesty."

King Lev looked over the written request carefully. In the past, he had simply signed and returned the application with scarcely a glance. His hesitancy and perusal now made Elior and Grace uneasy. Finally, he spoke. "Elior," he said. "You seem to be a trustworthy man who keeps a keen eye on the goings on in this city."

Elior nodded. No other response was expected.

"We have recently learned that the Princess of Novus has been kidnapped—taken by your son actually. His motive is unknown, and I am sure you know nothing of this."

Elior and Grace shook their heads, feeling and communicating in their expression a genuine surprise.

King Lev studied them critically. The severity of his expression lessened only slightly as he said, "The punishment for such an action is death—for your son and for anyone who aids him. Should he appeal to you for help, a vicious choice will be set before you. If you help him, it will be found out and you will all be killed without mercy. However, if you alert us to his presence and his plans, I can promise that your own lives will be spared and that you will be rewarded for your actions."

"We have not heard from him in many months, your royal highness," Grace said with a confidence and calm she didn't know she possessed.

The King nodded. Very slowly and deliberately, he signed the request and handed it back to Elior.

All this time, the Queen had remained silent, though she twitched nervously. As Elior and Grace turned to leave, she stopped them. "Please," she pleaded. "Please, if you are contacted, return my daughter to me. It has been many years since I have seen her and I am so worried."

Elior and Grace had to clench their fists and bite their tongues. After a few deep breaths, Grace turned to the Queen, looked her straight in the eye, and evenly said, "I understand, your majesty."

With a wave of his hand, the King dismissed them. As soon as they were out of the room, he snapped his finger. A tall, dark, spindly man instantly appeared. "Follow him," the King commanded in a low voice. "I want to know everything he sees, everything he does, everyone or everything he is with—"

The lanky man nodded and slunk silently out of the room.

Scarcely more than a few hours later—indeed as soon as all of the necessary arrangements could be made at the house, Elior and Grace left their home, each carrying a small bag. Grace rode upon their trustworthy mare, Dahara, while Elior walked along beside her. If one were to have watched especially close, one would have seen a couple of dogs slide out the door behind the exiting couple.

As it happened, one lanky man hiding in the shadows was watching especially close and there was not much his sharp eyes missed.

Although the mangy-looking dogs and the couple did not travel together through the city, they did end up at the same place: Elior's workshop. Elior hooked Dahara up to the cart they kept at the shop and loaded the tools. Before heading out, he scanned the route ahead of them, absent-mindedly scratching the fur of the dogs as he did so. Then the dogs and people parted ways again.

# 21

# TEMAN RIVER

When Elior and Grace arrived at the city gates, they
handed the guards their signed permission slip, hoping
for the same careless inspection they usually received.
Their hope was realized. The guard barely glanced at the paper,
nodded, and held it out for them to reclaim.

The document never reached their hands.

A long bony arm shot out of nowhere and snatched up the paper
before Elior could grab hold of it. At the man's appearance, the guard
became as disconcerted as Elior and Grace. He quickly retreated and
busied himself, or tried to busy himself, with anything else.

"Just another day in the woods is it?" asked the lanky man who
had grabbed the paper. His voice was slimy and full of sarcasm.

"Yes sir," answered Elior evenly. He knew as well as the guard
who this man was—Mêkar son of Moreth—the king's chief informant. Not only was this man an informant, but he had also been
given full power over the lives of anyone whom he suspected was in
league against the king. In other words, he was the king's swift judge
and merciless executioner.

"And taking your dogs with you, how very thoughtful," Mêkar
spoke again, his voice continuing in a falsely congenial tone.

The couple looked puzzled. "Dogs sir?" asked Elior.

"You must be mistaken," said Grace hurriedly. "You see, we don't own any dogs."

"Really?" Mêkar pretended to look confused. He shook his head as though he were trying to clear the mix-up, then stopped and looked directly at them, a small smile playing at the corners of his thin mouth. "No, I am sure I saw two dogs leave your house not too long ago. And then—let me see—yes, Elior, you were petting them and seemed quite friendly with them later at your shop. Are you sure they are not yours?"

Elior shook his head, trying desperately to remain as aloof as the man before him. "Just trying to show a bit of kindness to some poor, homeless animals, sir."

"How kind of you. Oh look, there they are again. They certainly do follow you about, though not directly, I've noticed, which is also rather strange."

One of the dogs stepped further back into the shadows at this attention. The other stepped forward, on full alert, its hair standing up on end.

"I say," continued the lanky man, pretending to look at the paper. "I have an inkling that the king would also enjoy the company of such worthy animals. I tell you what. I am willing to do you a favor and take care of these animals while you are on your outing. They would only be a nuisance to you. What do you say?" He held the permission slip tauntingly toward Elior. Elior wavered in indecision.

A flash of movement brought all further negotiations to a direct halt. One of the dogs had lunged at Dahara, causing her to rear and bolt recklessly forward. Elior and Grace, who had dropped hold of the reigns during the exchange with Mêkar, had no control over the mare and were forced to hold on to the cart for dear life. A bark from this same dog to the cowering one caused that frightened creature to bolt forward as well. The desperate mare plowed a path of destruction that Aliatta (for she was indeed the timid dog) easily followed.

Levi was a menacing canine and was quite successfully keeping the guards and Mêkar at bay. However, he could not hold them off forever. Before long he was surrounded and a sword pierced one of his shoulders. The wounded creature slammed desperately into one of the guards, giving himself enough of an opening to burst through the men and become lost in a sea of people and overturned carts.

Mêkar glanced disdainfully at the disorganized soldiers and then strolled casually after the disappearing dog, following a trail of blood.

Meanwhile, Darhara was galloping away as fast as any race-horse. After all, what horse wouldn't run away from that strange shiny creature who was chasing her? Emerging from Zion's gates, she bolted down the hill and flew across the miles of open plains. That thing kept pace with her, always just out of reach. Kings Creek slowed her pace only slightly as she splashed through the shallow waters. It wasn't until she neared the North Badali Forest that her gallop slowed to a trot, then to a walk. She stopped right at the edge of the trees. The creature had finally disappeared. Dahara looked back at her owners then as if to say, "Well, I got you here. Now it's your turn."

Elior and Grace climbed shakily down and, with fumbling hands, managed to unhitch the cart. Needless to say, little remained of what had once been in the cart. Aliatta soon caught up to them, panting heavily from her own frantic race through the countryside.

While Elior ministered to the needs of the horse, Grace gave her attention to Aliatta. It was a one-sided conversation, for although Aliatta could understand everything her mother said, she was only, at the moment, capable of communicating in dog language. It finally dawned on her that she could try spirit-speaking. After that, conversation flowed much better.

Aliatta had already grown tired of being a dog and was reasonably desirous of changing back. *I'd really like to be a girl again, but I think I'll need your help,* she told her mother.

Grace nodded and promised to help in any way she could, but before Aliatta could begin the process, her father came over and put a hand on her shoulder. Then he gravely pointed to the horizon from which they had come. A cloud of dust filled the air, indicating the presence of a large group of riders coming fast in their direction.

"We should hide the cart and move under the cover of the forest before we do anything else," Elior said, his brows furrowed in concern.

Grace and Aliatta agreed with question. Once the cart had been carefully camouflaged, Elior and Grace mounted Dahara, and they all disappeared into the dense forest. They traveled without speaking; their hearts pounded loudly within them. The slightest movement of forest life caused them to jump in alarm.

"This used to be my favorite place," Grace whispered, her voice full of regret.

While Elior's keen eyes and knowledge of the wood were engaged in seeking out a trail in front of them, Aliatta's attention was tuned in to the path behind—listening for the sounds of those who hunted them.

They had not traveled long in this fashion when Aliatta heard a rustle in the undergrowth not far behind. She instinctively froze, on alert, teeth bared, ready to confront the intruder.

Her heart nearly gave out when the canine form of Levi immerged. He was no longer the ferocious animal he had been when she'd last seen him. His body sagged and pain filled his big, brown canine eyes as he limped up to them. Those eyes met hers and he let out a shuddering sigh of relief. Looking carefully around, he painstakingly made the change back to his Adama form. The stress of the change caused blood to flow freely from the wound that cut across his right shoulder.

Elior and Grace gasped at the sight and quickly dismounted. Grace grabbed some extra material she had brought while Aliatta utilized her knowledge of forest flora to sniff out some helpful plants—in this case, garlic and yarrow. The garlic would serve to disinfect the wound while the yarrow would speed up the blood clotting process. Within a short time, the wound was dressed and cared for to the best of their limited abilities.

This task complete, Grace suggested they take a moment to rest beneath the cover of some nearby trees, but Levi shook his head and stood up.

"I would love to rest," he said wearily, "but we can't. Not yet and definitely not here. Dogs aren't the only bloodhounds—he's still tracking us and I'm afraid I've been inadvertently helping him."

"Mêkar?" Elior asked, correctly identifying the Adama bloodhound.

Levi nodded.

"The blood you lost," said Grace with a new awareness of the situation. "He's been following that."

Levi nodded again. "I know I shouldn't have come after you. I've probably endangered you even more this way, but … I didn't know where else to go."

"Of course you were right in coming to us," Elior said confidently, giving him an encouraging pat on his uninjured shoulder.

"So, where do we go now?" inquired Grace, shouldering her pack.

"*Would it be better for me to change back?*" asked Aliatta. She had remained admirably focused on the task of searching out the healing plants and had been equally successful in putting her own desires aside. However, now that they were talking about moving on, she really wanted to be an Adama again. She was also afraid that she wouldn't be able to make the transformation on her own.

Levi shook his head. "It would be even more dangerous for them to find and recognize you, Aliatta. Besides, your dog senses can still be a great help to us. We need your help; we need you to guide us now."

Aliatta's canine head dropped in disappointment and a little doggy whine escaped. "*What do I need to do?*" she spirit-spoke to him.

Levi talked her through what to look and listen for and how to use her senses to find the kind of shelter they needed. The plan was successful. Aliatta was able to find and guide them to a large, spacious bush. A bit of minimal crawling between the branches brought them all (except Dahara) to the bush's hollow middle. Its spacious center contained thick branches that curved and crisscrossed all throughout, creating a plethora of backrests and seating areas. Once inside, they sank into the ground or against the branches to rest.

Aliatta was finally given the go-ahead to change back into an Adama. This time, Levi merely said, "Ok, Aliatta. You know what to do." Then he leaned back against a branch and fell asleep.

This was not the response Aliatta had been expecting and it nearly sent her into a panic. How would she ever change back if he didn't help her? She ran round him in circles, pulled at his legs, breathed stinky dog breath in his face, but he didn't budge. With a final whine she gave up and found a little corner in the bush away from the others. After all, she didn't see any point in making her parents watch her awkward and inevitably failed transformation.

In less than fifteen minutes, Aliatta reemerged—a twelve-year-old girl once again. Levi was still sleeping and she glared at him as she passed by to talk to her parents.

Two hours later, after they had eaten and Levi had awakened, they discussed their next move. It was decided they would travel south to the Teman River, though they had no idea how they would get across.

"The High King has gotten us this far," Levi comfortably pointed out. "He'll provide a way for us to cross."

Though her parents seemed to accept that response easily enough, Aliatta did not possess such an easy confidence. However, seeing as how they had no better options, she decided to once again lean on Levi's faith. Maybe one day she'd possess more of her own.

One by one, they cautiously emerged from the bush, looking and listening for any sign of danger. Levi and Aliatta rode on Dahara while Elior and Grace jogged silently beside them. A couple of hours later, they reached the edge of the forest, a short distance from the river. A dangerous clearing was all that stood between them and the Teman.

Elior crept out into the open, looking this way and that for any sign of their pursuers. There were several moments of silence and then—

"Run!" he cried

Hellions were emerging from the trees to the west of them. Leading the menacing hoard was the dark, malicious Mêkar, coolly mounted on a fierce black horse.

Dahara reared and bolted straight back into the cover of the woods, her movement so sudden and erratic that she threw off her two riders. Now all four of them were on the ground.

"To the river!" cried Levi.

They were closer to the river than to their enemies, otherwise they may not have even attempted to outrun the monstrous Hellions. But run they did, though they still didn't know what would happen once they reached the river.

Mêkar smirked as he watched them run, waiting for just the right moment—

"What are you waiting for!" cried one of the Hellions.

Mêkar looked down with disdain upon the creature who had spoken. "Patience, creature," he said calmly. "Those pathetic fools are running towards a dead end. They have nowhere to go once they reach the water, unless they are planning to commit suicide by trying to swim across that vast thing. Let us wait just a minute longer and at least get some exercise out of this chase."

The Hellion said no more but furiously waited for the order. When the order came, it was not the order for a full attack. Instead of sprinting full force, they were ordered to jog—a demeaning order for Hellions.

Even with the slower pace of their enemies and the closer distance they had to the river, the evil behind our sprinting quartet was too close for comfort.

At the very edge of the water, they stopped. Aliatta and her parents suddenly realized that they had been expecting—something—to happen by now, but nothing had. Levi, however, threw a last glance over his shoulder and then, to the great wonderment of the others, plunged straight into the powerful river.

That is when the something they had been waiting for happened. As soon as Levi made contact with the water, it began to change. The waters separated and swirled about. Water from the east gathered and grew into a large wave. The wave curled over but didn't crash down. Instead, it stayed frozen in that curled position. Through the barrel of the wave, a tunnel emerged, leading down and through the vast sealike river.

Aliatta eyed the tunnel skeptically. "I may not know much," she yelled over the noise of the roaring water, "but I do know you can't walk on water!"

"You're right," yelled Levi with a teasing smile. "You don't know much! Come on!"

Aliatta and her parents looked at each other, shrugged, and jumped in. With every forward step they took, the water closed back over the place they had just been, leaving them in an astounding cocoon of water, surrounded on all sides by aquatic life.

Aliatta gazed in awe at the new view. Fish of every shape and size peered curiously in at them. When she looked down, she could see to the depths of the river and when she looked up, she could see birds soaring in the sky. Aliatta reached out a tentative hand and touched the sides of the water walls. Her hand made ripples, just as it would have if she had touched the calm waters of a lake. The water itself felt no different than the cold, clean touch of the river. Mist from the walls filled the air. *It's like I'm standing behind a waterfall,* Aliatta thought.

Out of curiosity, Aliatta looked back one final time to the bank she had left behind. Much to her amazement, she saw the cool and collected Mêkar throwing a wild tantrum while the Hellions howled with rage.

# 22

# THE LiViƏs

Aliatta arrived at the south bank of the Teman River exhausted and dazed, for even with a tunnel providing them an unobstructed path, it had been a long distance to walk. They had begun this leg of the journey when the afternoon sun was still high overhead, and now the moon shone down in its place. Granted, they had not walked the entire time, for Levi's wound had made it necessary to stop and rest at frequent intervals. In these moments of rest, the water had provided a nice, though relatively discomfiting cushion. I can't say that any of them were completely at ease with the idea of sitting or leaning against such a clear, flimsy looking wall. It was unnerving to gaze through the walls and see such a wide variety of river creatures, all looking as though they could plunge their mouths, or even their whole bodies, right into the little tunnel. Of course, none of the creatures even tried to penetrate the enforced barrier. All the same, even though it was the means to their salvation, the river tunnel had not been an easy or comfortable means.

So when someone on the opposite bank offered Aliatta a fist-sized branch to grasp onto, she gratefully accepted it and climbed out, not caring who it was that was extending the offering. Once her feet were firmly on the bank, she sank down and wearily looked up, expecting to see flesh at the end of the branch. What she saw, however, was more branch leading up to a solemn wooden face, above which was a head full of leaves and branches. The branch hadn't been the means of someone helping her; the branch had been part of the someone who was helping her—a Livid who stood a few feet taller than a tall man (measured up to the face, for that is how the height of a Livid is gauged by Adamas). And this Livid wasn't alone. Aliatta and the others were surrounded by what seemed to be a small family group—a grove of Livids.

In her groggy state, Aliatta absent-mindedly observed that her parents seemed just as dazed as herself. Then she looked for Levi. A small gasp of alarm escaped her lips as she saw him passed out on the ground nearby. Several Livids swayed and bent their branches round about him. Aliatta couldn't see what they were doing and this also concerned her.

"What's going on?" she asked of the Livid who had helped her up from the river.

The Livid looked at her with a calm, sympathetic expression. "Your friend is tired and wounded, but with the help of our herbs and a good amount of rest, he will be okay. I suspect that some rest would be good for you as well."

Aliatta nodded, her eyes heavy.

"My name is Bridgit Nightfall," offered the Livid pleasantly, bowing and rustling her leaves by way of introduction.

"I'm—"

"Lady Aliatta. We know. We have been watching for you. Our brothers in the North Badali forest—those few who are still secretly loyal—alerted us to your coming."

"How do I know I can trust you?" mumbled Aliatta. Mention of the North Bank had brought to Aliatta's exhausted mind a vivid remembrance of all they had just escaped from. Her safe, mundane

world of Earlington Castle had exploded and she didn't know who
or what she could trust anymore.

"Do you have the strength not to?" Bridgit's answer was soft,
almost like a lullaby.

"Not right now," the weary girl groaned.

"Then come with us. You will be safe, for a little while at least."
At a nod from Aliatta, Bridgit gathered the girl in her branches and
followed the other Livids into the heart of the forest.

***

Aliatta opened her eyes to a dusky light filtering in through the
leaves and branches of the bush where she and the others and been
taken to rest. As her eyes adjusted and her senses started to awaken,
she yawned, stretched, and slowly sat up. How long had she slept?
A nearby rustling alerted her to the fact that others were stirring as
well. Aliatta's progressing consciousness soon brought another ob-
servation. She could see her father and mother, but not Levi.

Levi was nowhere to be seen.

Her eyes shot open in fear. Where was he? Had the Livids failed
to heal him? Had he been in worse shape than they'd supposed? Had
she chosen the wrong plants for healing?

Mercifully, she wasn't given much time to fret over the worst
possible scenarios, for the next moment, Levi appeared. He cheer-
fully maneuvered into the hideaway, looking as fit as ever, though
his shirt was slightly bulkier around the right shoulder. He casually
handed each of them a bowl-shaped piece of bark filled with a variety
of berries and other plants before sitting down with his own bowl.

"How long did we sleep?" asked Aliatta, still trying to shake the
last vestiges of slumber from her body.

"Through the day at least," replied Levi. "Night is already approaching and I think I heard the Livids talking about moving on
once it gets dark."

Aliatta nodded without further questions—for the time at least—and the four of them ate in silence. Immediately upon finishing, the questions began in earnest.

"What exactly happened back there?" asked Elior.

"How did you know to touch the water?" inquired Grace.

"Where was the High King in all of this?" questioned Aliatta.

Levi looked to his right and seemed to be engaged in some kind of unseen conversation. Then he turned back to address them.

"The High King never left us," he stated simply. "He was there the whole time, and his servant Melhem was journeying with us that entire time as well."

"Then how come we couldn't see him?" asked Aliatta, a little upset that apparently she had not been deemed worthy enough to look upon the mighty messenger of the High King.

Levi shrugged. "Sometimes the physical situation demands all of our attention. For reasons of survival, we cannot always see both the physical and the spiritual simultaneously. To survive, we must sometimes focus solely on the physically present. Ultimately, though, it is the High King who decides when it is good for us to be able to see his messengers and when it isn't. So, in regards to what happened with the water, well, I was already physically tired and was finding it very hard to concentrate on physical things. So, I focused more on the spiritual things you couldn't see. Eventually I couldn't see Mêkar, but I could see the Erela, Melhem. I simply followed him into the water.

"There are also other reasons I know the High King was with us. Melhem was the one urging Dahara on across the plains. Aliatta, you thought that because I wouldn't help you make the change to Adama form, you were alone. You weren't. Melhem was right there with you, working with the High King to give you the thoughts and focus you needed. When we were crossing the river, I was tired, and my body would have given out much sooner had not the High King given me the strength I needed to make it to the other side."

As Levi had been speaking, Elior's eyes had taken on a faraway look, as though recalling some distant memory. "It has been many years since I have looked upon an Erela," he said softly, almost to himself. "Could I see him now?" he asked in a hesitant voice.

In answer, an iridescent, translucent form began to materialize. In a matter of seconds, Melhem was visible.

Elior gazed at him in wonder. In an almost apologetic tone, he said, "Now, perhaps you can answer a question I've had for years. I have always wondered: if the Dark One was created by the High King and was once the servant of the High King, how could he have gone so wrong? What happened?"

Melhem sighed in sadness at the memory. He seemed to be listening. Then he nodded and began the story.

# 23

# He Did Not Create Him to Be Evil

The change didn't occur all at once and, no, the High King did not create him to be evil. The High King created him to be what we are all meant to be—messengers of His word and a reflection of who He is. We were not created to be things that automatically obey without question. We were made with the ability to choose whether or not to obey the One who made us.

"I can still remember the first moments of my own awareness. As a newly formed being, I had looked around until my gaze settled on the glorious figure standing in the midst of us. As his radiance filled and reflected through me, I had slowly bowed my head in reverent awe to my great High King.

"With us now created, the High King turned his attention to the next items of his creation. Wisdom, joy, freedom flowed through him as land was formed—solid ground, dirt, and grass. Rushing rivers cut through the land and pooled together creating a large body of water. Hills and mountains thrust their way through the earth to tower above the rolling plains. Luscious trees and flowering plants colored the land in an artistic array.

"All the while, I had watched in expectant awe, catching the ever growing joy and excitement which was radiating through my maker with each new creation. Occasionally, we would shout with glee as some new plant would spring up and a bud would open to reveal a new wonder.

"This process continued for a long period. At some point, I decided to wander and explore the space we were in. Riding upon ribbons of light, I gradually worked my way towards another figure in the vast expanse of the heavens.

"'Hail, Commander Zohar,' I communicated.

"'Hail, Melhem,' he had replied without emotion, without excitement.

"I didn't understand his lack of enthusiasm for what was happening. 'Are there words, Zohar,' I said, 'to describe such wonders as the King is creating?'

"'No, Melhem,' Zohar had replied with a slight smile, 'but do you not agree, that as lovely as it all is, it pales in comparison to our own beauty.'

"I was stunned at this response of his, and Zohar could tell.

"'Come now,' he said with conviction, 'do not look so shocked. You know we are by far the most beautiful of his creations. But, yes, this land is very lovely and will do very well as a place for us to rule. I do wonder what my subjects shall look like.'

"As Zohar spoke, his light, very slowly, very subtly, dimmed.

"At this point, I noticed the High King had paused and was gazing in satisfaction at all he had created. It was good. I turned away from Zohar and joined my voice with the flowers, the trees, the hills, the mountains, the valleys, the rivers, the great water, and the other Erela. We lifted up our voices and sang.

"As glorious as everything was, there was more still to come. Excitement radiated through the High King as He explained to us the love He had for us and for those whom He was about to create. They would be given leadership and authority over the land, serving as He directed, for it was by serving him that they would best be able to serve each other and the land over which they were being made the caretakers.

"Zohar, however, seemed not to be listening as the High King laid out his designs. 'And now for my subjects,' he quietly hissed.

"I looked at him curiously. His eyes had taken on a dark expectancy.

"'Just watch, Melhem,' he said. 'These slaves will do my every bidding.'

"I glanced askance at Zohar. 'Didn't you hear the High King, just now?' I asked. 'His next creations are to be his subjects, not yours, and they are the ones who will be given charge of this land.'

At this point I noticed something very disturbing about the light within my commander. With every passing minute, it seemed to grow more and more dim. 'Zohar!' I exclaimed in dismay. Perhaps he was unaware of what was happening. 'Zohar, your light—'

"'My light, Melhem,' he said, 'is my own.'

"I realized then that my Chief Commander was fully aware of what was happening. In the pride and arrogance of his own importance, he was more and more ceasing to reflect the light and goodness of the One who had made him. I turned away, not knowing what to do and not wanting to watch his descent into darkness.

"I turned my attention again to the workings of the High King. It was a wonder to watch as He created such an astounding assortment of creatures. When He finished, He spoke with select members of each group, teaching and instructing them.

"Then the High King spoke to the Erela and gave us our assigned task.

"'You know how much I love you,' He said, 'Never doubt my love. I have a very important role for you. You are strong, of body and of spirit. These other races are not so naturally strong. They will have great need of your services. To you, I am giving the task of protecting and serving these other races, especially the Adamas.'

"'Were we not good enough?' growled Zohar through his teeth.

"I had nearly forgotten Zohar's presence, but his voice reminded me that he was still there. 'Commander,' I said desperately, 'surely you heard the King. He loves us.'

"'So he says,' was Zohar's bitter reply. 'But how do we know he is telling the truth. If he loves us so much, why isn't he making us the kings? Why does he subject us to be the slaves of such weak creatures?' Zohar's anger rose with every syllable and with every syllable, his light faded.

"Then, suddenly, his expression softened. He looked at me kindly. 'Don't you see, Melhem, he doesn't really love us. He loves those weaklings. Look at me. Look at us! Do you really believe such strength was created for nothing? Do you really believe our magnificent forms are meant for nothing more than to be that of errand boys? No, Melhem, we were made to be rulers!' By now the voice of my Commanding Erela had a soothing, melodic tone. 'You see, Melhem, the High King is tired. He has been working very hard and was confused when he spoke to us. That's all, just confused. He meant to say that the Adamas will serve everyone and that we will be the rulers.'

"I hesitated. The words sounded so true, so logical. Zohar was strong, and he was beautiful. I began to doubt and to think that maybe the High King had made a mistake. Maybe he had gotten confused and meant for things to be the other way around.

"Then I heard another voice speaking to me. 'Melhem,' it said, 'never doubt my love. Hold tightly to what you know is true.'

"'My King?' I asked.

"'Yes, my loved one, it is I,' spoke the High King.

"The light and life of the High King pulsated through my body. There was no doubt now to whom my spirit was aligned.

"'I believe,' I said softly, but loudly enough for my darkened companion to hear.

"'What?' yelled Zohar.

"'I believe the words of the High King.' This time, I spoke with confidence. I looked again at the one whom I had considered to be my commander and noticed something more strange than anything I had yet seen. 'Zohar,' I said, 'your light is hidden from me.'

"All pretense suddenly disappeared from the mighty Erela. He was, in fact, shining forth darkness—a darkness which appeared as a sharp stain in the heavens. Eyes glowed fierce and he moved as though to strike me. At the moment of the assumed impact, however, my light shot out from all directions, momentarily blinding my now darkened Commander.

"Cursing, the Dark One fell back and shot off into the distance, screaming as he did, 'I am not finished. Just you wait! I was made to rule and I will rule!'"

***

"What happened then?" Aliatta's voice broke into Melhem's memories.

Melhem didn't answer. He had stopped for a reason, though he wasn't sure yet what that reason is. And then he knew. *I'm afraid story time is over,* he said. *Look, the Livids have arrived to guide you on to the next phase of your journey.*

Sure enough, a young sapling was climbing into the bush. "It is time for us to escort you to the edge of the forest," he announced loudly and with some importance. His eyes shone with excitement and it was obvious he was quite delighted with the role which had been assigned to him. "My family and I will take you to the edge of the forest where you will be met by a specially chosen family of Pronghorns. We must travel very quietly," here his voice dropped low, "through the woods, for not all the Livids, even in this area, are on our side."

The group nodded, gathered their things, and silently followed the young, important Livid.

# 24

# THE PRONGHORN

The night had arrived with a thick blanket of clouds which stretched across the heavens, hiding the light of the moon and stars and wrapping the forest in a protective darkness. With the darkness now serving as their ally, the company of Livids and Adamas traveled swiftly and undetected through the South Badali Forest.

Had it been light, and had they not been on the run, Aliatta may have enjoyed walking through this dense northern forest. She may have noticed the lush green leaves of sugar maple trees. She may have gazed in awe at the contrast provided by the white trunks of the birch trees and the silver-gray bark of the beech trees. Unfortunately, all she could see were the dark outlines of numerous trees, passing by one after another.

Hours later, the group arrived at their destination on the southern edge of the forest. Here they were met by a family of elk-people. Their bodies were like those of an elk, but from the chest on upward, they were human. They did, in fact, look very much like centaurs, with the exception that from their heads protruded a light and intricate arrangement of horns.

There were nine Pronghorns in this particular family group. The largest, who was apparently the group's chief, stepped forward to speak with Eamonn Moonkind, the Livid elder. Aliatta's father,

Elior and Levi were invited to join the discussion as well. The others of the Pronghorn family, seven adults and one child, hung back. The adults kept a keen eye on the surroundings while the child stared at the Adamas in unbridled curiosity. The darkness, however, made staring more difficult and far less interesting. Therefore, it wasn't long before the young elk-child scampered right on up to Aliatta.

"I've never seen an Adama before!" she whispered in awe. "It must take *forever* to get places with only two legs to walk on!"

An older Pronghorn, who was apparently this young one's mother, turned abruptly from her surveillance duties in dismay.

"Sitsi," she reprimanded in a loud whisper. "Don't be so rude! That is no way to talk to the Princess!"

Sitsi's eyes widened in dismay. "I'm so sorry, Princess! I didn't know you were the princess. I thought the princess would have beautiful clothes and her hair would be done in all kinds of pretty ways and—"

"Sitsi," cried her mother again in shock and embarrassment.

Aliatta laughed quietly. "It's okay," she said. "I wouldn't recognize myself as a princess either. Right now, I am simply a wandering girl who is trying to follow the directions of a High King whom I barely know."

The elk-mother smiled. "We welcome you with honor anyway, wandering girl. Come," she said, noting that the meeting of the elders was breaking up. "Ride on my back for this first part of the journey. As my precocious child pointed out, it is much faster to travel on four legs than on two."

Aliatta readily accepted the offer and hoisted herself up upon the elk-mother's back. As the elk-people sprinted off into the darkness, Aliatta vaguely noted that the shapes of the trees had disappeared and been replaced by other shapes. She strained her eyes in an attempt to better see her surroundings. Her eyes, however, were as tired as the rest of her and she soon fell asleep.

\*\*\*

Aliatta awoke to the soft glow of the rising sun. The earthy fragrance of fresh grass surrounded her and drifted in through her nostrils. A muted rustling sounded beneath her as she stretched and moved her head from side to side. Tall grasses loomed high above her in all directions. She reached a hand down by her side and grasped a handful of thick, spongy grass. Although the makeshift bed was soft enough, her body felt stiff. *I miss my own bed*, she thought as she stood up in an attempt to work out some of the kinks. Rubbing the sleep from her eyes, Aliatta surveyed her surroundings. They seemed to be in some kind of shallow ravine. Hills rose up on every side, decorated by boulders of all colors, shapes and sizes. The tall grasses were interspersed with understated wild flowers. She smiled in delight as understanding dawned. They were in *her* hills—the rolling hills of Alsta—and the land was even more beautiful than it had appeared from the castle window.

The two hundred mile journey to their midway stopping point in Darnstall hold passed pleasantly in its own way. This isn't to say there weren't dangers (at least half the Pronghorns were always on alert), but for all that, it was a smooth journey. Aliatta used these days to practice transmogrifying herself into the likeness of a Pronghorn. This exercise was a treat not only for Aliatta, but also served as entertainment for the others of the group as she worked through the awkwardness of learning to move and function as the Pronghorns did.

"You're right," Pronghorn-Aliatta called out once as she raced Sitsi across an open hillside. "Having four legs is so much faster than having two!"

"Then why don't you stay with us like this for *always?*" asked Sitsi, who rather liked the idea of having a playmate.

Aliatta came to a stop. "I can't," she said thoughtfully. "As fun as it is to be like this for a while, it isn't who the High King made me to be. He has something else in mind for me, though I'm not exactly sure what."

"When will you know?" questioned Sitsi in awe. Everything about Aliatta fascinated her, and she couldn't *imagine* not knowing what you were made to do.

"I don't know the answer to that either, Sitsi," responded Aliatta softly. "But I think the answer is one of the things this journey is supposed to show me."

In addition to transmogrification practice, these days of travel also provided a much needed opportunity for Aliatta and her parents to get to know each other better. It was a bit tricky sometimes, trying to figure out how to interact. Aliatta had always been rather independent, and the responsibilities of this situation, as well as the nature of the situation itself, were serving to mature her at a much faster rate. What then was her relationship to her parents to be? It seemed strange to ask them for permission to go play, and yet disrespectful not to. Her parents, too, were hesitant and reluctant to request things of her or to offer correction. Levi was the only one whose treatment of her remained constant. Their relationship continued to be what it had always been—that of tutor to student.

As the days went on, Aliatta and her parents slowly found themselves opening up to one another. Her parents would share their experiences and Aliatta would find herself drawn into the lives of these people who seemed so familiar, and yet so foreign. Her own world widened as she listened and took hold of the wisdom they shared. Aliatta soon discovered she finally had people to whom she could openly and unreservedly share her heart. Thoughts, questions, dreams, and emotions she had never felt safe speaking about with the Duke and Duchess came flooding out. With each thought and experience she shared, her mother would empathize and provide an in-depth analysis of the emotions going on within those involved while her father would lay out the bare truth of what had been happening in those moments. In this way, Aliatta came to see her parents as people whom she could trust to provide her with truth, insight, and wisdom; and her parents came to understand their responsibility in guiding this growing-up princess in the way of truth.

The days of travel were so pleasant that Aliatta was almost disappointed on the day they were to arrive at Darnstall Hold. The thought of an inn, however, did serve to stir up some excitement within her. Although her body was becoming more accustomed to sleeping on the ground (there was less stiffness when she woke up in the morning), Aliatta was relishing the idea of a night spent in a real bed.

Their approach to the bustling settlement was a quiet one. It was to be their first venture into a populated area since Zion, and though it would be dangerous, both Levi and Elior felt it was necessary in order to gain information on the state of things, namely—how much knowledge of them had spread and where the forces of the Dark One were located. It was agreed that the Pronghorns would stay hidden in the hills outside the city while the four Adamas made their way to the inn of a loyal one.

And so, under the cover of darkness, the four well-intentioned fugitives traipsed toward Safehaven Inn where a small white candle glowed dimly in the darkness. It was after midnight when they arrived and their steady knock was met by a large, grumpy man who was none too pleased to be bothered at such a late hour.

"May the King live forever," greeted Levi softly, looking the man directly in the eye.

"And his light never be extinguished," returned the man with a sigh, his cranky expression lessening somewhat to one of sorrow. He looked them over as carefully as he could in the dim light. "Four of you—," he said slowly. "You should know, there are agents of the King here, and I don't mean the King that lives forever. They have been here for a couple of days now—looking for a group of four Adamas—I'm sure that wouldn't be you, though."

"If it was," said Levi slowly, never breaking eye contact, "what would you do?"

"I have a wife and child of my own," answered the innkeeper with some reluctance. He looked down, no longer able to meet the gazes of those who had come to his door for help. "I'm afraid the best I could do for them would be to suggest that they make their way from Darnstall Hold as quickly as possible."

"We see." Elior stepped forward and spoke without emotion. "In that case, we must beg your pardon for having troubled you. Good night."

As they turned away, Aliatta looked back, mourning the loss of a comfortable bed. Her eyes accidentally met those of the innkeeper and he turned away in shame.

*It's okay,* she wanted to say. *You've turned your back on us, but it doesn't mean you have to turn your back on the High King altogether.*

She watched with a sinking heart as the innkeeper shuffled heavily over to the candle and blew out the light. An inexplicably heavy sadness filled her soul. A comforting hand touched her shoulder and she looked up to seeing Levi's understanding eyes gazing into her own.

*Have hope, Princess,* Levi said, spirit-speaking into the sadness. *The Innkeeper may have given up on himself and on the High King, but the High King has not given up on him. Above all, hold on to the hope that he may again light that candle.*

Unbeknownst to the Adamas, their brief and silent exchange had been witnessed. Dark eyes peered out of the windows of another inn nearby before disappearing as silently as they had appeared.

"Quickly, over here. Now!" Nakai, the Pronghorn chief.

The dejected Adamas looked up in alarm to see Nakai the Pronghorn chief urgently beckoning to them from the shadows of a nearby building. With him were three other Pronghorns.

"Your presence here is known," he told them once they were all gathered. "We came as soon as we could. The innkeeper is no longer counted among the loyal ones."

"We know," sighed Aliatta.

"I'm afraid things are even worse than that, Princess," said the chief. "A hoard of Hellions arrived a week ago and have taken up residence within this settlement. One of the Dark One's servants was at the inn across the street. He saw you speaking with the innkeeper and has alerted those foul creatures to your presence. They are on your trail even as we speak."

"What's the plan?" asked Levi, his mind instantly switching to action mode.

"You will ride upon our backs onto the open roads. Once the Hellions have seen us and are in pursuit, we will ride to the eastern edge of the settlement. There, we will meet up with the other half of the Pronghorns. They will ride on in the direction of the sea, making it look as though they are the ones who are carrying you. Meanwhile we will double back and continue to head in the direction of Redford Palace."

"Why doesn't the High King just—zap them away or something?" asked Aliatta. After all, she thought, He had blinded the eyes of those at Earlington palace so she and Raz could escape. He had created a tunnel in the midst of the water. Why didn't He just do something like that again?

"He has already helped us and will continue to help us," answered Nakai in all seriousness. "Who do you think gave us the idea in the first place? Sometimes the High King provides help through miracles. Sometimes He helps by the plans He reveals and the strength he gives. Now come. We must go at once."

The Pronghorns, with the Adamas mounted upon their backs, raced in and out among the shadows of Darnstall Hold. Nakai led the way. He always seemed to know exactly what to do at just the right moment. Aliatta lost track of the number of close calls. Arrows whizzed by on all sides and there were too many times when the wind of a Hellion claw could be felt as it narrowly missed either herself or Nizhoni, the young Pronghorn maiden she rode upon. Once outside the settlement, they quickly gained ground across the grassy knolls, then made a sudden turn. This change of direction brought them to a hidden cave where the other Pronghorns waited. As soon as they arrived, the other four adult Pronghorns, each loaded with a large, Adama-size bundle, galloped off in the direction that the Hellions had last seen them going.

Nakai motioned for them to keep still as he listened for evidence of what was happening outside. Then he motioned to Sitsi who cautiously crept out of the cave. When she returned a few moments later, she nodded to the Pronghorn leader. The Hellions had taken the bait and were in fervent pursuit of the decoys.

The Pronghorn chief led his charges through the cave to a back exit which emerged just south of the city. From here, they continued on their original course, heading southwest towards the village of Wintertide which rested in the foothills of the Icy Mountains.

The journey from Darnstall Hold was not at all like the journey to it had been. For one thing, the land was completely different. Gone were the hills with their protective ravines and large boulders. In their place were miles upon miles of flat, open plains—the agricultural district of Novus. Golden-hued wheat rose high above the ground, moving in waves like an ocean when the wind blows. An endless azure sky reached down and wrapped the land in an all-encompassing embrace. Clouds of all shapes and sizes floated carelessly in the heavens above, drawing imaginative gazes from any below who cared to look. For the leisurely traveler, this land was an undisturbed joy to travel across. However, our travelers were not of the leisurely sort. They were in a desperate race to save their lives. So instead of being a land of spacious beauty, the open plains became a place of grave danger. The tall crops gave them occasional cover, and the level ground made it easier to spot trouble far off, but for the most part, our friends were pushing hard to make it across the treeless plains without being captured.

Aliatta found herself wondering if it was all worth it, and if she would ever again have the luxury of sleeping in a real, full-cushioned, silky-sheeted bed.

# 25

# THE KEEPERS OF THE GEM

It was a weary group of travelers who carefully made their way beneath the shadows of Redford Palace and down into the level valley which was home to the tiny community of Wintertide. The days through the shelterless plains had been long and rough. Sitsi had long since lost her joyful little bounce, Aliatta had ceased changing into other creatures—it took too much energy—and even Levi seemed more tired in spirit. This exhaustion increased with every step, for, after the disappointment of Darnstall Hold, each traveler had their doubts about entering even a sparsely populated area.

Their spirits lifted only slightly when they arrived at a stone well on the edge of town, then sank again as they gazed at the village—or what they could see of it anyway. From their place at the well they could see the full width of tree-high hedges which surrounded Wintertide and served as the settlement's only wall. These leafy barriers were thick and provided outsiders no opportunity to catch even a glimpse of what might lie within. Not even the smallest of openings was visible. The group looked at each other in dismay. Entering the settlement might not be an option after all.

For now, though, they at least had water. The Adamas went to work lowering and filling the bucket for the Pronghorns before

tending to each other. Once this task was complete, they sat down
with a sigh against the stone walls of the well. Only then did they
notice a young lady in a simple green dress who was staring at them
with sympathetic grey eyes.

Elior was instantly on the alert. There was no telling who could
be trusted. He pulled himself up as quickly as his tired body would
allow and then he and Nakai approached the woman—to greet her
and, more importantly, to assess whether or not she posed a threat.

The woman smiled knowingly, almost as if she guessed their in-
tent. She spoke quickly before they could offer their veiled greeting.
"Please, fair travelers. I wish you hadn't felt the need to get up. You
face no threat here and you are tired. Please, let the waters of this
well refresh you and then come with me to my father's house. You
may stay with us for as long as you have need before continuing on
to your journey's end."

Elior and Nakai looked at each other uncertainly. They looked
to the others of the group as if to say, "Can we trust her?" The others
shrugged, clearly having no more insight into this than they did.

Finally, Elior spoke. "May the King live forever," he said mean-
ingfully, looking her directly in the eye.

The young woman looked confused, though her eyes never left
his. "I suppose some may wish that to be the case," she said in a matter-of-fact tone, "but nobody lives forever. For now, though, I would
be honored if you would come to my home and stay with us." She
hesitated and then admitted, "There are others there already—more
than a dozen Adamas, but between my family and our neighbors,
we always find room for everyone."

At this proclamation, the ears of all the travelers perked up and
they sat a little straighter.

"This group," said Levi, "is there a man named—"

"Don't!" interrupted the woman sharply. She shot them a look
of warning. "We don't know their names. We never ask the names
of those to whom we offer shelter and protection. We find it better

not to know, so please don't tell me your names or ask the names of the others. I only ask that you come with me and allow my people to help you."

The group, however, remained where they were, still uncertain. Could something like this really be trusted? The young woman seemed honest and sincere enough, but was she only pretending so as to lead them into a trap?

In the midst of their uncertainty, two familiar faces walked onto the scene—Rosemary and her granddaughter Marnie.

Aliatta stared at them blankly. Her interaction with the family had been brief and she had been taking in huge amounts of new information. Therefore it is understandable that she didn't even remember little Marnie. Levi, however, knew immediately who they were. While Aliatta was still racking her brain to figure out why they seemed so familiar, Levi jumped up to greet them.

After some hugs and general inquiries into the well-being of the others who had come with Rosemary, Levi finally got around to asking where she and the rest of the group were staying.

"Didn't Atira tell you?" asked Rosemary in surprise, gesturing towards the young woman they'd just met. "We're staying with her. Well, with her and her neighbors."

"But can they be trusted?" asked Elior doubtfully. "After all, she didn't know the sign."

"There are things these people do not know," acknowledged Rosemary, "but there is much they do know as well, and you can rest assured that they hear Him and act according to his ways, even if they do not yet know his name."

Elior nodded, then turned back to his wife. Grace had been staring hard at Rosemary. Suddenly, she came forward with a gasp. At the same time, Rosemary also recognized her old friend and the two women met in an embrace. It took Elior longer to recall the acquaintance of nearly ten years ago, but when he did, he too stepped forward with a hug.

And these hugs were only the beginning of the reunion hugs. The small group, both Adamas and Pronghorns, followed Atira, Rosemary, and Marnie to the small community where everyone was staying. Wintertide was an intriguing town in that the placement of the homes, shops, trees, rocks, and roads had all been designed in such a way as to create an intricate labyrinth within the protective shrubbery surrounding it. Atira moved through the maze without a thought. Rosemary and Marnie didn't seem bothered by the layout either. For the newcomers, however, it was more than a little disconcerting to realize that they wouldn't be able to find their way out if they wanted to.

After many twists and turns, they finally arrived in the center—a clearing which consisted of five long wooden houses placed end-to-end in the shape of a pentagon. At the announcement of their presence, people excitedly emerged from each of the houses and the reunion hugs resumed. Introductions were made, though it was a tricky business trying to introduce and be introduced without stating a name. They soon discovered that the people of Wintertide were rather proficient at getting along without knowing the names of their guest. You see, they came up with their own descriptive names for each person such as: Serious-eyes (Raz), Esteemed-One (Raziela), and Caterpillar (Aliatta). There was a great feast following these greetings, after which everyone happily retired to their own, or designated, homes.

Elior had been able to arrange things such that he, Grace, Raziela, Raz, and Aliatta were all together in one residence. It was the first time in his life that he had ever been able to be with his mother and children all at the same time.

Taking the first opportunity he had, Elior warned Raz of his name being known and informed him of the charges which had been laid out against him.

Although Raz had suspected as much, it was still hard to hear the verbal confirmation of his suspicions. After all, for a man, the loss of respect in a job he has worked long and hard at is never an easy thing to bear. So the displaced knight looked at the floor with a heavy sigh and, with a wry smile, murmured his regret. "A decade of loyal service to the King and Queen and this is how it ends—"

"But which King were you really serving," Elior pointed out. As much as he wanted to support his son, there was no time to wallow in self-pity.

Raz nodded and he thought deeply about the honest question. His spirit revived somewhat at the opportunity to be put his analytical mind to use. "It was easy to forget, to lose sight of why I was really there," he said. He turned his contemplative eyes to his sister. "Aliatta, though you weren't aware of it, you helped me, more than anything else, to remember what my true purpose was. Well, I guess this warrant for my arrest would explain some things."

"Like what?" asked Aliatta.

Raz shook his head. "It's late," he said, "and you are tired, little caterpillar. I'm sure you will hear many stories in the days to come."

Raz, as was often the case, turned out to be right. The next few days were ones of rest and recuperation, and Aliatta did indeed learn the "like what" events which had prompted Raz's comment.

"Raz taught me how to fight!" exclaimed Giron one day to Aliatta as they sparred together with small, sleek rapiers. "I've even been in a real battle!"

"Really?" asked Aliatta with some surprise and more than a little skepticism.

"Well, it wasn't a real big battle," acknowledged the boy, "but it was a real fight! We hadn't traveled very far from where you left us when we stumbled right into a camp of Zobeks! You should have seen me! Quick as lightening, all of us, well, almost all of us— Raziela and Marnie hid in a tree—grabbed our swords and sent those pesky ape-monsters running for the hills!"

Another day went by. Seventeen-year-old Maya joined Aliatta for some time away from the general populace. They had found an irresistibly great climbing tree close to the village clearing and were now expertly perched in its high branches.

"There was one time when we barely avoided running into a trap that had been set for us," Maya softly recounted. "We were on the high ground, surrounded by large boulders, but were about to approach a clearing. Raziela suddenly stopped us from moving forward and suggested we go back down the hill and around through the ravine before coming back up. None of us wanted to climb any more hills than we had to. We were tired of the constant ups and downs and wading our way through the higher brush in the ravine, but we listened anyway and went around. After we emerged on the other side, I looked back to where we would have gone and saw a group of Adama bounty hunters waiting to catch us. It's a wonder they didn't hear us and snatch us up anyway!"

# 26

## TRUST

One evening, Raz shared some more details about their journey. "We would make our way from home to home—homes of those whom Ian and Rosemary knew to be trustworthy," he explained. "We were hidden in all sorts of ways, in all kinds of places—beneath floorboards, under hay, in the rafters of homes and barns, in half-full barrels of wine, secret compartments of wagons— Each time I thought we were sure to be discovered, the soldiers turned away. Something would divert their attention. I don't even know what it was that drew them away."

"Sure you do," responded Raziela with a knowing smile.

Raz smiled in return. "You're probably right," he agreed. "Something inside me did, I think, have a sense of what was going on, but I never saw the help that was given. My training has taught me to be highly alert and aware of the physical. I don't think I've learned yet how to be aware of the spiritual. I always suspected though, that you, grandma, always knew exactly what was happening. This trip has been strange in another respect as well. As a knight, I've been accustomed to always knowing who is in charge, but on our journey, it was never clear which one of us was doing the leading. We led together, it seemed—Raziela, Ian and Rosemary, and I. And, there was one more thing I found strange. Some days into our journey, the attention of the Hellions seemed to have been diverted for good. They had been tracking constantly, but suddenly they stopped. I can only assume now, based on your own story, that it must have been when they turned their attention to Darnstall Hold."

They had not been long with the people of Wintertide when Aliatta discovered some blank parchment in one of the homes. After gently fingering it and staring at it longingly, its owner, Maor—Atira's father and the leader of Wintertide, offered to give her some.

"Do you mean it?" she eagerly asked, her eyes bright with hope.

Maor nodded with a smile. "I always have as much as I need," was his simple reply. Then he handed the girl a pen and a small jar of ink to go along with the parchment.

Aliatta gratefully accepted the offered gifts and shot out the door. Then she seated herself at one of the tables in the center of the clearing and began to write. As she wrote, her mind left the village of Wintertime and went back—back to her bedroom at Earlington where her adventure was about to begin. Pen touched paper, and the journey began again.

She had not been writing long before she had a silent audience. First it was only Sitsi, coming over to see what her friend was doing. Then Giron, Henry, and Marnie showed up, and then Sean and Zavier sauntered by and loitered there, trying not to look as interested as they really were. Before long, there was a whole group gathered around the young Lady Aliatta who was so absorbed in her writing that she wasn't even aware of their existence. Raziela looked on from the outskirts of the group with a smile. This was indeed her granddaughter.

A bell finally chimed, announcing the noon meal, and Aliatta looked up, her mind slowly returning to the present. She was more than a little surprised to see so many faces staring back at her in awe.

"What are those marks you were making?" asked Sitsi in wonder.

Aliatta did her best to explain sounds, letters, and words and finally, exasperated by having to explain something which was so easy for her now, blurted out, "Maybe I should just start at the beginning and show you!"

"Yes!" the group exclaimed.

They were called for lunch before Aliatta had any further chance to respond.

Over lunch, Aliatta explained to Levi the horror of the situation. "I don't know why I offered to teach them how to read and write. I didn't mean to! Levi, why don't you teach them? You're the tutor, not me."

Levi smiled as he gently, but firmly responded. "Believe it or not Aliatta, they look up to you, even the older ones. They know who you are and have great respect for you. There comes a time when the student is called upon to step forward and teach, and for you, that time has come."

"But I know so little." Aliatta sighed. Managing a prison was one thing. Teaching others what she knew was something else entirely.

"There is much you don't know about the High King," Levi agreed, "but there is much you have been taught about the world He created—things that these people have not yet had the privilege and opportunity to learn. No, you don't know everything, but what you do know, you are able to share with others—to teach them."

"Will you help me?" she implored.

Levi nodded. "I will be there with you and will lend you what strength I can, but I will not do the teaching for you. Remember, too, the High King will give you the energy and words for the task. You already have the knowledge, so proceed with confidence. You are not alone."

Thus began the daily lessons. Every morning, the Heir to the throne of Novus would come out to the clearing and teach, not only the children, but also many of the adults, how to read and write.

Through Lady Aliatta's offering of the knowledge she possessed and the students' grateful acceptance of her gift, a bond was formed and mutual respect was exchanged. Aliatta's eyes were opened to the beautiful and wonderful qualities of those whom she had previously viewed as being beneath her, while the community discovered, in this young aristocratic girl, a generosity and friendliness they had not expected to find in someone who had been raised among the nobility.

The days at Wintertide passed pleasantly, but alas, this was only a temporary stopping point and their rest here could not last forever. After a few weeks had gone by, Raziela, Levi, Raz, Ian and Rosemary, and Elior and Grace met to discuss the next phase of their journey.

"I would highly advise against traveling through the White Country," Ian said fervently.

Raziela looked confused. "I don't understand why," she said pleasantly. "It is such beautiful country. I passed through there often in my younger days."

"I'm afraid much has changed since then." His tone softened in response to Raziela's good memories of the place. "They say a heartless Ice Witch now rules the country. While she doesn't appear to support the Dark One directly, she does not tolerate people entering into her domain. Skerps are tolerated, but only because they do her dirty work for her by gobbling up anything that dares to pass through. It is said she can look into the souls of those who trespass onto her lands and freeze their hearts to solid ice. It is said she flies upon the wings of a Chashak and moves as silently through the forest as a Pronghorn. Her own heart, it is said, is made of ice. Even the Hellions dare not go there, for she seems to have an especially strong hatred of them and will turn them immediately into the worst thing she can think of."

"Which is—" prompted Raziela skeptically. She had never cared for gossip and this description sounded rather far-fetched.

"A harmless white daisy which instantly freezes and dies in the cold air," said Ian, completely serious.

Raziela laughed outright, but the rest of the group gave a sigh of frustration. To go around the White Country would add significant time and danger to their journey, for they would be much more vulnerable out on the plains which lay along the borders of Alsta and Ebrodon.

They left the meeting still uncertain as to what their next course of action should be. As it was, before the night was over, their route would be decided for them.

***

*DONG, DONG, DONG DONG*

The alarm sounded soon after everyone had retired for the night.

"Wake up everyone! Rise to your feet! The enemy is at our doorstep!" shouted a man who barged into the room where they were sleeping. In a matter of seconds the door slammed shut as the man moved on to the next house. Raz sprang to his feet, threw on his leather armour, sheathed his sword, and helped get the others prepared.

"What's going on?" Aliatta whispered to Atira.

"A hoard of Hellions has arrived and surrounded the village. We don't have much time. Quick, follow me."

Atira and the rest of the hospitable people of Wintertide led their Adama guests to hidden doors beneath their floorboards and ushered them through. The Pronghorns could not fit inside these flaps. Instead, they found places to hide within the labyrinth itself. Then the leaders of the community went out to meet the enemy.

Levi tried to warn the Wintertide residents that the Hellions would not negotiate with them.

*Please don't go!* he spirit-spoke to Maor as he walked out the door. *You cannot reason with those monsters.*

Meor looked back with calm, understanding eyes. *Do not fear for us,* he said, spirit-speaking in kind, *for the Hellions will not harm us. The people of Wintertide are under the special protection of King Lev and Queen Malka. You see, the King and Queen entrusted us with something very important, very beautiful, and very dangerous. They have entrusted us with the Gem of all Knowledge. And now you must go, before one of them sees you.*

While the leaders of Wintertide spoke with the Hellions and told them all the things they did not know (We don't know whom you are speaking about. We don't know where they came from. We don't know where they might be going), the very people for whom the Hellions were searching were making their way through hidden tunnels beneath the feet of those who hunted them.

The Adamas walked and walked and after a while the tunnel began to slope, leading up and up and up. Finally, they could go no further, for the simple reason that there was a door in the way. They pushed and pushed, but could not force it open.

"Why don't we knock?" suggested little Marnie.

Most of the group was split between thinking she was cute for suggesting such a simple idea, and thinking she was just an ignorant child not to be taken seriously. Marnie only shrugged. *That's the polite thing to do when you come upon a closed door,* she thought. While the others lingered in indecision, Marnie marched right up to the door and knocked as firmly as her six-year-old fist could knock.

"Oh my, Ranaan, we have visitors," came a cheerful voice from the other side of the door.

"Do you think it's safe, grandpa?" a young voice asked.

"Of course. Nothing of darkness would come through *that* door, and if it did, it certainly wouldn't have the courtesy to knock. But

I will check, just so you can rest at ease. May the King live forever," the first voice called to them.

Raziela gave a broad smile as she stepped forward to answer, "And may His light never be extinguished, Orel."

The rusty door opened and Raziela embrace her old friend, Orel—the scribe to whom she had entrusted her original manuscripts.

After introductions were made, this time with real names, they set about the task of learning where exactly they were.

"You don't know?" he asked in surprise. "Ah, yes, I do remember that passage to be rather confusing. Well, my friends, you are in the Icy Mountains of the White Country."

And so their route had been decided. Orel described the path they must take and even drew a map for them. Then he and his grandson took them to the outer door of their hidden cave and said good-bye.

The travelers soon missed that modest, cozy cave. Outside, a cold wind was blowing with such energy that it would pick up the snow on the ground and send it whirling about them.

With words of encouragement and cheer to one another, they began their journey through the White Country, one step at a time.

# 27

# THE ICE WITCH

T here is something about a trek through the mountains, isn't there, Aliatta. Nobody in search of a life of ease would willing choose such a painstaking way." Raziela's words came haltingly in labored breathing. She was certainly not as young as she used to be and the many uphill climbs were proving to be more taxing than she wanted to admit. "It is a constant journey of ups and downs, usually with more uphill climbs than downward ones. Sometimes you get so focused on putting one foot in front of the other that you lose sight of all the beauty surrounding you. You forget why you are on the journey in the first place. And then you come to a break in the trees—a place on the edge of the mountain that gives you a wide view of everything beyond. The beauty, the wonder, the majesty suddenly hits you and you realize that this upward journey is making you stronger—bringing you higher, taking you to a place you have never been. The journey is worth it."

Aliatta gazed at her grandmother with an affectionate smile. They were now on their third day of hiking through the Icy Mountains and the journey, though "worth it" as Raziela had said, was taking its toll, especially on the older woman. It was, in fact, her weakening state which had prompted them to stop early on this day to rest at the edge of a high clearing where the view was indeed an awe-inspiring one. From this vantage point you could see all of White Country and beyond. Half frozen rivers, huge jagged mountain peaks, and beautiful snow covered fir trees littered the countryside.

Raziela's aged body shook as she sat resting on the ground with her back up against a large pine tree. Her eyes, in contrast to her body, shone brighter than anyone's.

Levi and Raz set about getting a fire going and then settled Raziela close by. The rest of the frozen travelers also huddled around the welcome warmth and rested there all afternoon.

Raz stayed next to the fire only long enough to get his blood flowing again and then left with Sean, Zavier and Reut to scout out a good place to camp for the night.

By the time evening arrived, the weary travelers were making themselves at home beneath the overhanging cover of a large boulder.

Long after the others had fallen asleep and the coals of the fire glowed with their last hint of red light, Raziela lay awake, her spirit troubled.

"What is it," Raz asked quietly, stirring slightly beside her.

Raziela shook her head. "I don't know," she whispered. "With all the beauty of this land, it feels dark—cold—some places more than others. It feels so different from what I remember it being. There is anger in the air, and right now that anger is strong."

Raz became instantly on the alert. "What exactly are you sensing right now?" he asked. He had now been with his grandmother long enough to know better than to take her "feelings" lightly.

"Anger, hatred ... wicked glee?"

"And that feeling is stronger than usual right now," Raz reiterated, his eyes peering intently into the darkness beyond their camp. "Grandma," he said slowly, "I think you are picking up on the spirit of some very unwanted guests—Swords! Everyone! Now!"

The rudely awakened group had just enough time to grab their swords and form a protective semi-circle around the opening to their shelter before the silhouettes of a hoard of Skerps appeared before them in the moonlight.

The hoard rushed forward, screeching in excited glee. Swords clashed and the sound of steel hitting steel rang out across the mountains.

The swordplay among the Adamas had, as a whole, certainly improved and for a long while they successfully kept the attackers at bay. Gradually, however, the younger and less experienced members of the group began to tire and as they did so, they retreated into the shelter with Raziela and Marnie. The fight lasted through the night. By the time dawn began to signal its approach, only Raz, Aliatta, and Levi remained fighting. Raz and Aliatta used their swords quite effectively while Levi fought in the form of a large bear.

The Skerps, however, outnumbered them greatly and Raz found himself evaluating their chances of survival to be growing smaller by the minute. Just when Aliatta felt she could hold out no longer, they heard a loud, terrifying yell.

"Stop!" a voice thundered.

It was a cold, harsh voice and the sound of it echoed through the mountains. The Skerps completely froze and then scurried away in a whimpering retreat.

The Adamas breathed a collective sigh of relief and exhaustion. Their relief, however, was short lived, for the source of the voice which had caused the Skerps to cower was coming fast upon them.

At first it looked like a cloud rolling soundlessly down the mountain. Then they realized that the cloud was really snow—a silent avalanche cascading down the mountainside, heading directly towards them. Most of the group wisely huddled beneath their shelter, but Aliatta stood just outside it, watching in awe as the avalanche drew nearer. At one point, she rubbed her eyes, sure that she could not be seeing what she thought she was seeing, for what she was seeing was this: in the midst of the cloud of snow was the figure of a tall, slender woman—her white hair and grey raiment billowing around her in harmony with the tumultuously tumbling snow.

"The Ice Witch," breathed Levi. He had transmogrified back to an Adama and was also standing outside the shelter, as mesmerized by the sight as Aliatta. Fortunately, good sense took hold of him immediately after he spoke and he thrust both himself and the Lady Aliatta beneath the shelter of the large boulder.

The ice and snow careened silently and harmlessly over their rock and when it cleared, the woman who had been riding within the cloud was standing firmly before them. She was tall, though not abnormally so, with long white hair that fell wildly down her back and across her shoulders. She wore a long-sleeved gown of grey fur. Fitted down to the waist, the gown then billowed out in layers all around her, giving one the impression that she was always moving or floating above the ground. Her face, however, was by far the most noteworthy aspect of her appearance. It was young-looking in the sense that there were no wrinkles, but it was a hard, sharp, angular face. The mouth held no trace of a smile and the eyes—they were fierce and dark, so dark in fact that they seemed to be without pupils. These eyes surveyed them and nearly all of them shuddered with the intensity of the inspection. Raziela was the only one not affected in that manner.

While the others shuddered and cowered, Raziela shook her head in disbelief. "Could it be," she muttered under her breath.

Before the Ice Witch, for it was indeed the Ice Witch, could utter a word, Raziela hobbled out from among the crowd and gave the woman a tremendous hug. "Elsie, my friend!" she burst out joyously. "Let me look at you." She stepped back and observed the woman. A sense of wonder filled her eyes. "Why, you look as young as ever!"

For the first time in many, many years, the Ice Witch was caught off guard. Her mouth opened in surprise and a look of pain rushed over her face. Even those black eyes seemed to shine a little less dark.

"Ra- Raziela?" she stammered. "How ... how are you still alive? I was sure the Dark One would have killed you by now—you and everyone else who still followed the High King."

"Oh, Elsie, the High King is so much more than you've ever given him credit for being. Look at us. Look at all of us. We are all servants of the High King and he has kept us very much alive, though—we are very tired at the moment."

The Ice Witch Elsie looked, really looked, for the first time at those who gathered behind her old friend. Surprisingly, her gaze softened and her angular features looked a little less sharp. "Come with me, then," she said. "There is a place close by where you will be warm and safe." She turned, clearly expecting them to follow, and as she did so, she ignored for the first time in a long time the Chashak who stood by her side advising her against such hospitable actions.

# 28

# THE LOST PRINCESSES, ELSIE

L ess than half a mile south of where their overhanging rock shelter had been, Elsie turned off the path, navigated smoothly over and around some large boulders, and then slipped sidewise through what looked merely to be a large crack in the mountain. The others were none too sure about following this questionable ally into such an unknown shelter and so they lingered by the opening until Raziela and Raz caught up to them (it had taken Raziela much longer to maneuver around the large rocks, even with Raz dropping back to help). Raziela took one glance at their wary faces and then moved without hesitation through the large crack. Raz immediately followed and then the rest of the group did likewise, though with far less confidence. After a few feet of sidewise movement, they were amazed to find themselves in a large, spacious circular cave. Furs lined the perimeter, both on the floor and on the walls, giving the place quite a cozy feel. A large fire glowed and flickered in the middle of the cave. Elsie sat watching their arrival from a raised rock ledge on one side of the shelter. This ledge, as well as the walls around it, had been covered with fur, making it look as though she were sitting on a fur throne while her subjects entered meekly into her presence.

Once they were inside, Elsie, with a rough jerk of her head, motioned them over to one of the rugs on the far side, opposite from where she sat (they didn't dare disregard her command). She then proceeded to study Raziela and her family closely. Everyone else was casually ignored for the time being.

"Elsie," spoke Raziela in the same congenial tone she had first used upon seeing her old friend, "I would like you to meet my family: my son Elior, his wife Grace, and their children Raz and Aliatta. Family, this is my old friend Elsie, the one I have often told you about—the lost princesses of Novus."

The family smiled kindly and Elsie found herself giving a rusty smile in return, though she offered no words of acknowledgement. She felt a peace, a gentleness, a kindness among these people. It was a familiar feeling and she recognized it as the spirit she had always admired in her confidant of so many years ago. With a pang in her own spirit, she realized just how much she had missed it.

"Elsie," spoke Raziela again, emboldened by her friend's smile, if not by her silence, "I've always wondered, what happened to you after you left?"

Elsie's eyes took on a distant look. "I have not thought of that time for many years, my friend," she said sadly, "but if anyone deserves to hear my story, I suppose that person is you. I was upset, as I'm sure you remember. I didn't know what to think or how to feel. I was angry and scared. I ran out of that castle as fast as I could, having no plan, no idea of where I was going. I only knew I had to get away—away from the evil masters who were trying to control us. As I left the city gates, I was stopped by this Chashak." She gestured over her right shoulder and seemed to be listening to something. Her eyes narrowed and although her facial expression never altered from that of annoyance, her gestures indicated that she was immersed in conversation.

"What are they saying," Aliatta whispered to her grandmother.

"I don't know, my girl, and it is good that you are not picking up on the conversation either, though I'm sure you can feel the spirit of it. It is best not to try to attune yourself to the voice of the Dark One, for in doing so, it becomes more difficult to hear the voice of the High King. By the way—as long as she is not paying attention to us, listen carefully to my warning: it is imperative that Elsie does not learn you have been selected by the King and Queen as her replacement—"

Elsie turned back to them, the annoyed expression still on her face. "Anyway, this Chashak, Casimir, stopped me on my way out. He was writhing in the most pitiful way. When he saw me running away from the castle, he begged me to take him along.

"'I thought you served the Dark One!' I yelled. I didn't even glance at him as I ran on by. He kept pace with me, however, whining and assuring me he had no allegiance with the Dark One. 'What about the High King,' I demanded. 'Why don't you run to him then?' At this suggestion, he shook even more.

"'No, not the Terrifying One! Anywhere but him! Don't make me go back to him!' he pleaded in absolute horror. I couldn't believe how desperate he sounded. 'He's even scarier than the Dark One!' Casimir continued. 'He would do all kinds of terrible things to punish me!'"

"He would do no such thing," interrupted Raziela. "Elsie, if you believe those words of the Chashak then truly, you do not know the character of the High King. If Casimir, or you, were ever to desire to return to him, He would welcome you gladly."

Elsie's gaze softened as it always did when she looked at her friend. Her eyes took on a wistful shine. "Your sincerity almost makes me believe it, my friend," she said. "But I am too far gone at this point for either the High King or the Dark One. In these mountains, I am Queen."

Raziela opened her mouth to respond, but another voice chimed in before her thoughts had opportunity to be heard.

"What happened next?" prodded a wide-eyed Aliatta. She had

already been drawn in to the story and I am sorry to say that her question was ill-timed.

Elsie smiled and continued. "Well, I finally stopped to listen to the poor creature. 'What do you have to offer me in exchange for allowing you to accompany me?' I asked.

"'Long life,' said he. 'I can give you long life, make you look young forever, and make you stronger than you've ever been before' he said.

"I agreed and we sealed the deal, creating a bond between us which can never be broken."

"What did you do?" Raziela asked in a low voice. Alarm shone through her eyes. Of all her friend had told her, this was by far the worst—to form such a bond with a Chashak was indeed a dangerous business.

Raziela's alarm was by no means lost on Elsie. Her eyes turned defiant and she responded harshly. "It is of no concern to you, oh *elderly* one. Though you were my friend and I consider you one still, you are no longer my advisor and therefore the means I have used to get where I am now are of no concern to you either. You always were very judgmental, Raziela. Anyway, after our bond was made, Casimir led me here, to these mountains. I have spent the last eighty years building and expanding my power and influence. Now, every creature I allow to live here is under my power. The Skerps fear me and do exactly as I command. The Hellions do not dare to cross my borders."

"If that is so," broke in Ian coldly, "then would you mind telling us what *that* thing is?" As he spoke, he gestured towards the cave entrance.

They all looked. Standing large and ominous against the wall next to the entryway was a Hellion.

There was a second of stunned silence before Elsie burst into action. In one fluid motion, she moved to the fire, picked up a flaming log, and threw it at the intruder. The moment it made contact with him, the log exploded into a thick cloud of fire and smoke.

"This way!" she yelled. They immediately jumped up and followed her as she led them down tunnel after tunnel through the mountain. The weaker members of the group soon tired and had to be carried by the stronger ones. Raz and Raziela came last, their eyes and spirits alert to any threat which might be following them. They emerged from the mountain on a steep, rocky hill which sloped steeply downward until it made contact with the pastureland at its base.

"Go!" Elsie commanded once they were out. "Those two trees at the entrance of the valley mark the border of my realm. There is a forest to the north and a small settlement to the south. Both should offer you protection." She turned to Raziela who had made her way over to her friend as soon as she'd been able. "It was so good to see you, my old friend," Elsie said in all sincerity. "Truly, I wish you the best."

"Look!" yelled Raz, pointing up at the mountain from which they had just emerged. A lone Hellion stood high upon a rock. His bow was raised and aimed directly at Elsie. A second later, he released the arrow and Elsie fell to the ground. It was not the arrow which had knocked her down, however, but Raziela—and it was from Raziela's back that the arrow protruded.

"*Quickly, this way!*" they heard a voice cry. Elior and Raz picked up Raziela and followed Melhem down the hill and into the forest while Elsie unleashed a fury of fire and ice upon the entire mountain in retribution for the injury done to her friend. Then she turned and followed the group into the trees. A short distance into the forest, the ground opened, taking them to a hidden, underground burrow. It was the home of a family of Pronghorns—large chipmunks who spoke and thought with Adama clarity.

The Pronghorns had already pushed the beds together by the time they entered. Raz laid Raziela down gently and stepped back.

The rest of the family stood close by while Rosemary and a couple of the Pronghorns tended to the wound. Elsie paced restlessly. Everyone else found an out of the way place to sit as they nervously awaited the outcome.

"She's alive, but fading fast," squeaked one of the Pronghorns after a quick assessment of the patient.

Elsie stopped in her pacing long enough to bark out, "Why doesn't the High King do something? Doesn't he know this is one of his own?"

They were quiet as her question penetrated deep into their souls. The voice that answered was not one they had been expecting to ever hear again.

"He did do something," rasped Raziela in labored speech. "He led me to you, Elsie. He gave me one more opportunity to show you how much He loves you and wants you to return to him."

The room was completely still as Raziela turned her head in search of the next person to whom she knew she must speak. Her gaze settled on her son and the force of it drew him nearer the bed. "Elior," she said, "The High King has led you in ways I never could. Continue to trust him to guide you and this family. They will need you more than ever now—"

Elior nodded as he squeezed her hand in promise to look out for their family. Then he stepped back.

Raziela's eyes roved about once again and finally came to rest upon her granddaughter. "Aliatta," she said, her voice now barely discernible, "There," she whispered, pointing a shaky finger at her small bag of possessions, "there ... in that bag is the full copy of the story so far ... from the beginning ... add to it ... add this journey to the tale ... and grow ... always be growing ... in wisdom, beauty, and truth ... Aliatta, you are my descendent—" Her words died off as her face took on a softness and peace unlike anything they had seen before. Her fading eyes brightened and shone as they stared at something in front of her, beyond her … and then her physical body moved no more.

Everyone was still; tears ran down the faces of many of those present. Each found themselves busy with their own thoughts—their own emotions—

For the first time in nearly eighty years, Elsie didn't know what to do or how to feel. Love, hate, fear, anger, sadness, remorse, guilt, longing, envy—all these feelings and more coursed through her in reckless abandonment, uncontrolled and unrestrained.

Standing next to Elsie was Aliatta. As Raziela's life had moved on to another place, Aliatta had stepped back to stand next to this beloved friend of her grandmother's. She reached over now and timidly touched Elsie's shoulder as she spoke. "She cared very deeply for you. Please, come with us. Come with us and learn about the One she served. I don't know very much about him either. Maybe … maybe we can learn together."

Elsie's gaze softened and she looked longingly at the young girl who reminded her so much of her friend. She could feel herself wavering. She almost wanted to accept the offer—to go with these people who were so closely connected with the only one who had truly loved her and had proven her love to the very end. She almost wanted to, but then—

*The High King killed her*, she heard a familiar caustic voice whisper. *He sent her to you and killed her—he only wants to cause you pain.*

Elsie shut her eyes as the words of the Chashak ran through her mind. It was all so confusing. Who was the High King? Was he the good, kind ruler who could be seen through Raziela's love, or was he an evil vindictive being, as bad or worse than the Dark One?

*Raziela must have been deceived*, whispered the voice persuasively.

*Yes*, Elsie thought, *that must be the case.* To acknowledge otherwise would suggest that the last eighty years of her life had been in vain—the deal she had made to be of a horrible and fruitless nature. These thoughts were too much for her to bear. No, it had to be the

Chashak who was right and these mere people who were deceived. The Ice Witch shook her head and stepped away from Aliatta's touch.

"I won't serve such a cruel master," she said, angrily spitting out each word. "But serve him if you will. You will learn the truth about his character sooner or later. I pity you all for how much you are deceived. And it is because of this pity and because of my friend Raziela that I tell you to go now. Leave my presence. Flee to Brance. I will send my Skerps to protect you, but know this—if you or anyone else dares to trespass onto my land again, they will die!"

Ian wasted no time following these orders and immediately began readying the group to leave as soon as possible.

Elior and his family, however, remained unmoved as a wave of sadness and loss rushed over them. It was as though they were experiencing another death. Elsie had come so close. "Please," Elior said, holding out his hand towards her. "For my mother's sake, please come with us."

With tears running down her face, the Ice Witch shook her head and her eyes narrowed as she spit out her final words to Raziela's family. "I will never serve the one who killed my friend." Then she turned and stormed out of the hideaway to carry out her last display of affection for her old friend—her Skerps would protect that family with their lives.

"Don't you see," whispered Elior before he led his family out the door, "you have already been serving the one who killed her, and now, you will serve him deeper still."

Sir Raz and Grace were the next ones to exit. Finally, only Aliatta lingered with the Pronghorns in the little home where Raziela's body lay. With tears running down her cheeks, Aliatta collected her grandmother's bag. Shouldering both it and her own pack, Aliatta turned and walked out the door.

# 29

# Sorrow, Swift, Battles Fought

The dark, rocky plains of Ebrodon looked as though someone had taken a chunk of the mountain, crumbled it up, and sprinkled its crumbs across the level ground. It was by no means the easiest terrain to even walk across. And this heartbroken group was not walking over the rocks, but running, scarcely aware that a strong wind had swept them up from below, carrying them slightly above the loose gravel with a speed they didn't otherwise possess.

Aliatta moved through the world as if in a dream, scarcely able to discern what was real and what wasn't. Her grandmother's final words to her ran through her mind again and again, *"You are my descendent ... you are my descendent ... you are my descendent ..."* What did that even mean?

One fact of which Aliatta was vaguely aware was that they were receiving help from multiple sources—some seen, some unseen. Her father had taken heart to his mother's last words to him, and so, trusting in the guidance of the High King, he had soon set to work dividing the leadership and responsibilities. He and Levi led the Adamas across the rocky plains, keeping their eyes and spirits on the alert for any danger ahead, while Raz and Ian served as the rearguard. The slight shimmering of the air at their flanks gave evidence to the presence of Erela traveling with them, guarding and surrounding them on all sides; a hoard of Skerps followed at a slight distance—never nearer than a hundred yards. Unlike their previous interactions with Skerps, these Skerps were not pursuing them or trying to hurt them. They were instead, as the Ice Witch had promised, fighting off the Hellions who were indeed in deliberate and malicious pursuit.

The frenetic race continued all that day and well into the night. Much to their great relief, the treacherous gravel eventually gave way to smooth, fertile soil. The ground gently rose until it became a series of low mountain ranges with a very obvious road winding its way through the large rocks that peppered its surface.

After what seemed like forever, Elior and Levi halted next to one especially gigantic rock. They circled it and discovered an un-occupied hollow center. It wasn't until they were all gathered inside that they realized they could no longer hear the sounds of either the Skerps or the Hellions. It appeared, for the time being, that they were safe and alone.

Though not completely alone, thought Aliatta, for as they settled into the cozy refuge, the glow of several Erela began to appear. Thes Erela guided them to beds of soft mountain grass and gave them food to eat, ministering to their weary bodies and exhausted spirits. With this host standing guard, the Adamas drifted peacefully to sleep.

They awoke the next morning to discover fifteen mustangs munching on the vegetation right outside their cave. Faran's children were perhaps the most excited. Giron, Henry, and Marnie ran amongst the horses, enthusiastically claiming first one, then another, as their personal pets. The horses gave a whinny of acknowledgement to the children, but for the most part, kept eating. Finally, Faran and Kamila called their children over to eat their own breakfast.

# 30

# THE CITY OF BRANCE

They journeyed through Ebrodon on horseback. Giron rode with his father, Henry rode with his mother, and Marnie rode with Aliatta. The wind which had carried them along so quickly the first day was gone. So too, were the Skerps and, by all indications, the Hellions. The host of Erela, however, continued their vigilant guard around them.

These were quiet days. Raziela's passing weighed heavy upon them and they knew the danger had by no means disappeared forever. The land of Ebrodon, however, has a way of soothing those who are troubled and in search of peace. As the refugees rode beyond the boulder fields, they entered into lush forests where vibrant flowers and leafy vines flowed over every available surface. Gurgling streams called out their happy existence to the travelers while cascading waterfalls invited them to bask in their own exuberant life. It was indeed difficult to be disheartened in the midst of this vivacious land and the group soon gave into its happy call. Spirits lightened, bodies relaxed, and peace entered in.

It wasn't until the end of their second week of travel, when the stone walls and towering castle spires of Brance appeared on the horizon, that their previous fears reemerged. They wondered what the city would be like. Would they receive rest there, as they had at Wintertide, or would it be a place of peril, as Darnstall Hold had been?

The next day found them nervously approaching the long causeway which would take them up and into the city itself. Before they could step out onto the road however, Elior led them behind the shelter of some large rocks off to the side. For a moment, they all sat gazing up at the city before them. There was no doubt that this was indeed an impressive and intimidating place. Built into the upper part of a rocky mountain, the city loomed high above its surrounding landscape. The protective outer walls had been fashioned from the mountain itself and within these barriers, the city rose in accordance to the natural lay of the land. The castle had been built atop the highest point and could be seen for miles around.

The travelers looked at each other in doubt and trepidation.

"Do we dare move forward?" Raz asked silently.

Elior didn't know. He closed his eyes, trying hard to listen. Finally, he spoke. "This is not a decision I can make on my own," he said. "We must be in agreement. Raz, from the training you have received in calculating danger, what do you think?"

"I don't know. Maybe that is what worries me. I know so little about this city and its people. When it comes down to it, I guess I don't really sense any danger, only fear that something might go wrong."

Elior then turned to Grace. "What does your spirit tell you, my dear?" He asked his wife, looking deeply into her eyes.

"It feels fine," she answered simply, amazed at how much peace she was feeling.

He nodded and turned to Ian and Rosemary. "Do you sense any danger?"

They shook their heads. "I'm afraid I don't know anyone from this city, but I think I remember hearing that it's a nice place to live," offered Rosemary weakly.

Ian nodded in agreement. "The tradesmen from there are known far and wide for their excellent craftsmanship."

Bit by bit, the tension among them began to fade.

"Aliatta," her father said suddenly, as though something had just occurred to him. "Have you ever met the Duke and Duchess of Brance?"

"Umm …" her brows furrowed in thought and then her eyes widened in remembrance. "Yes, I have! It was a couple of years ago. They passed through on their way to Zion. They seemed okay to me then. The kids, Dedrick and Adina, were really kind, more so to me than I was to them, I'm afraid."

Elior nodded in satisfaction before turning finally to Levi. "Levi? What have you seen with your Second Sight?"

Levi answered without hesitation. "I've seen a host of Erela traveling with us everywhere we've gone. The High King will not abandon us now. I think we should proceed to enter the city."

Elior sighed. "I guess it's settled then." With nods and murmured assent from the rest of the group, he steered his horse around the corner and onto the wide stone road which wove its way up to the city gate.

While the exterior walls of the city were an intimidating sight, meant to discourage any would-be attackers, the interior of the city was pleasantly different. The moment Aliatta stepped through the gate and onto the cobblestone streets of the city, she was met by an onslaught of the most beautiful smells. Elaborate gardens were interspersed among the buildings made of sweet-smelling Rosewood. As they rode on through the streets, they passed by the shops of bakers whose delicious aromas drifted into the streets. Aliatta saw leather workers and wood carvers who were busy shaping their craft, sending earthy smells swirling and dancing among the other aromas. The streets of Brance were full, but did not feel overly crowded. People of nearly every race smiled as they walked along the roads, and only very rarely did anyone bump into another.

Aliatta was so absorbed in the sights and smells of the place that she didn't see the familiar faces until they were almost upon them. Before she could think to turn her head away or find a place to duck into, she heard a voice cry out.

"Aliatta, Lady Aliatta, is that you? Surely, it can't be, but it is!" Everyone on the street froze as three stately figures brought their horses to a halt directly before Aliatta and all who traveled with her. The girl who had spoken was taller than Aliatta by several inches. Her brown hair was intricately styled atop her head and she wore a beautiful light blue riding habit which served to bring out the rich tones of her tanned skin.

"Wow," breathed Marnie from where she sat on the saddle behind Aliatta, "so that's what a princess looks like when she isn't running away." Aliatta grimaced and turned to shush her little friend.

The Lady Adina didn't see the uncomfortable grimace of her friend, for she had turned to her parents, the Duke and Duchess of Brance. "See Mother, I told you it was her!" she exclaimed.

Aliatta, seeing there was no use pretending otherwise, summoned up what dignity she could in her travel-worn state and approached the lordly family to offer up the appropriate greetings.

"Aliatta, whatever are you doing here?" the young lady asked once the courtesies had been exchanged.

"Looking for you, of course," sang Aliatta with a practiced smile. "You see, I'm … I'm on vacation." Aliatta's confidence began to falter as she realized she couldn't come up with a viable, safe reason for her presence in the city. "I've—come to see you, actually, and—" Aliatta searched desperately for anything that might help her out of her current predicament. Her eyes settled on her brother. "You remember Sir Raz. He is, of course, serving as my bodyguard."

Raz took the hint and rode purposefully forward to stand protectively beside the Lady Aliatta. He had also met this family and, though he agreed with Aliatta that they seemed nice enough, they couldn't afford to let their guard down.

"Really?" Lady Adina asked, an eyebrow cocked in doubt. She didn't seem to be buying Aliatta's explanation. Her eyes narrowed as she looked carefully at the young noble, then at those around her. There was whispered conversation between the noble family and then the Duke of Brance himself rode forward.

Aliatta found herself growing more and more nervous and unconsciously started backing her horse up. Raz remained in his protective position, his hand resting lightly upon the hilt of his sword, alert and ready to spring into action if the situation called for it.

The Duke ignored him and instead looked directly into Aliatta's eyes. "We would like to welcome you, all of you, to our city of Brance," he said. "May the King live forever."

Aliatta's eyes brightened and she gave a quick gasp before answering. "And His light never be extinguished," she said hurriedly, her face relaxing into a smile.

Lady Adina rushed forward, her face beaming in delight. "Come," she exuded. "You must all come. You are our guests and are very welcome."

# 31

# HARBORING

It was an impressive party that made its way through the streets and up towards Braewood Palace. The Duke and Duchess rode at the head, followed by Lady Adina and Lady Aliatta, with Marnie who was having the time of her life. These girls were followed in pairs by the fourteen other horses carrying the sixteen other people who had been traveling with the Princess. All in all, it was quite the parade and nearly everyone in the city stopped what they were doing to watch.

When the assembly arrived at the castle, each individual was welcomed and treated with the highest regard. New clothing, made of the finest leather, was generously distributed.

Swords of the highest quality were given to Elior, Raz, Ian, Faran, Benicio, and his teenage sons Sean and Zavier.

"What about me?" asked Aliatta with envious eyes as she watched each of the men receive their weapons.

"Your skills are by no means inferior to theirs, my lady," said the Duke, bowing his head to her, "but your days of fighting with a sword are passed, at least for the time being. There are other things you will be engaged in learning and I'm afraid a sword would only serve to distract you."

The twins, Reut and Maya, were each given a bow and quiver of arrows.

"With practice, I believe these will suit you better than swords," the Duke said with a knowing look.

Grace was given a selection of the most beautiful plant dyes.

Rosemary, Kamila, and Livna were each given cuts of the most valuable plants in Brance.

Giron and Henry were given wooden swords, and Marnie was given a puppy. "Take good care of him and he will stay by your side no matter what," said the Duchess with a smile.

In addition to the new clothes, Aliatta was given a collection of scrolls. "Many races pass through these gates," explained the Duke. "These scrolls contain stories and wise sayings from each of them. May the study of these documents aid you in your service to the High King."

As for Levi, he would, at first, accept nothing more than the new clothing. "I have no use for a sword," he stated casually. "I have other means of defense." He did show an interest in the documents Aliatta received. This prompted the Duke to show him the library. After meticulously perusing the options, Levi chose a couple of scrolls and tucked them carefully away.

Once everyone had received their gifts, they were taken to ornate bedchambers where they were able to wash away the dirt and grime of their past travels. Cleaned up and clothed in new garments, they made their way down to the dining hall where a large banquet had been laid. They feasted long into the night and slept late the next day.

The sun was already high overhead when Aliatta awoke. She lay still for a while, relishing the soft, luxurious feel of the silk sheets. Now this was the kind of bed she could appreciate waking up in. It would have been tempting to lay there for the rest of the day had her stomach not growled, reminding her that many hours had passed since last night's meal. With a reluctant sigh, she got up, dressed carefully, and made her way downstairs in search of food.

Aliatta arrived in the dining hall to discover that most of her companions were on the same time schedule. Some appeared to have just been seated, others were coming in with her, and still more could be heard making their way down the hall. She gazed at the table fully laden with savory dishes. It seemed they had awoken just in time for the midday meal.

It was a merry group who gathered around the table, chattering and laughing as they ate. Aliatta found herself enjoying her surroundings in a way she had not done since Wintertide. They were about halfway through their meal when the door to the dining hall burst open and a rough-shod young man came careening into the room.

"Father!" he cried. His light, sun-bleached hair was windblown, giving evidence to a desperate ride, and his brown eyes blazed as he rushed over to the Duke.

"Yes, Dedrick, what is it? What did you find in your wanderings?" asked the Duke, quickly and accurately assessing the nature of his son's alarm.

"Hellions, Father! Headed this way from the north—a large hoard of them—larger than any I've ever seen!"

"Aliatta, this is due to your presence here, I presume," said the Duke gravely, but not unkindly, as he turned to face her.

Aliatta lowered her eyes. "I'm afraid I was not entirely honest with you about my reason for being here, my lord," she said.

"What?" responded Lady Adina in mock indignation. "You mean you didn't come all the way from Earlington just to visit me?" The Lady's eyes turned gentle. "Do not worry, my friend. We knew the High King had sent you here and that was all we needed to know for the moment."

"What we need to know now," said the Duke, "is where He has directed your journey's end to be. If it is to be here, we will guard you with our life. But if your journey's end is to be elsewhere, then we'd better help you be on your way as soon as possible."

Aliatta bowed her head in a gesture of humble thankfulness. "My journey's end is elsewhere," she said. "It is to end, I am told, in the valley of the Loyal Ones, but I do not know where that is. Levi has been my tutor and guide throughout this journey. If it pleases you, I need him to show me the way."

"Of course he must go with you," the Duke agreed. His gaze swept over the rest of those who sat at the table. "We will need help," he said to them, "so if you are willing, I would appreciate your service in assisting us with the defense of this city. We must hold off the Hellions and give Aliatta time to escape."

"I offer you my service as a strategist and swordsman," spoke Raz without hesitation.

"My family and I offer you our services as well," spoke Benicio. Sean and Zavier cheered at this pronouncement while his wife Livna smiled bravely.

"My sister and I offer our service, too, my lord," said Reut.

The Duke nodded. "It is well. It is well, too, for Elior and Ian to take their families and accompany Aliatta to the valley of the High King. Elior, I can see the conflict waging within you, but you have been separated from your daughter long enough. Now your place is with your family, as is Ian's and Faran's, for though Faran is strong, his children are young and they need him as much as your daughter needs you." The Duke turned again to look at his son. "How long until they arrive?"

"Nightfall for sure."

"Then we'd better get busy—as soon as we finish our meal. It may be the last full meal any of us will be able to enjoy for a while. Adina, once you have finished eating, go with Aliatta and help her prepare for the journey. I will send servants to attend the others who will be leaving. Livna, you will go with my wife. She will show you where you can be of service. Sir Raz, you will come with me. Everyone else will follow Dedrick to the armory. We *will* be ready." The room lapsed into silence after the Duke's instructions. The merry spirit of the meal had disappeared. In spite of the Duke's suggestion that they finish eating, nobody was hungry any more. Bit by bit, the members of the company excused themselves from the table and moved to do as the Duke had directed.

It was quiet in the room where Adina was assisting Aliatta with her travel preparations. Though the girls did not know each other well, a fast bond had formed between them and they were now feeling the loss of the coming separation.

"Take these," Adina said abruptly, handing Aliatta a pair of leather pants. "They are not the most glamorous things, but they are stretchy and comfortable and will make it easier to travel … And here, take these." She handed Aliatta a handful of blank parchment. "I've heard you like to write," she said by way of explanation. "Oh, and take these." Here she produced a beautifully embroidered box. "It contains our most rare and effective healing plants."

Aliatta smiled, grateful and touched by the generosity of her friend, but inwardly hoping the kind girl would not give her anything more to carry. To her relief, she didn't.

A knock at the door momentarily interrupted the travel preparations. Raz entered and walked slowly across the room to where they stood, his travel bag laying across his shoulders.

Aliatta looked at the bag, confused. "Are you going with us," she asked hopefully.

"No," he said, shaking his head. He put the bag down and wrapped his little sister in a big bear hug.

"I can't believe I'm going to be separated from you again!" she cried.

He hugged her tighter still and then released her to arm's length. "Look at me, Little Liat," he said. "Don't forget that this day, this battle, belongs to the High King. Trust and hope that you will see me again. I will come and find you at the first opportunity. But right now, I must stay and fight. It is what I have been trained to do and now, I can fully use my abilities in the service of the High King!"

Aliatta nodded, tears still in her eyes. "I understand," she said, surprised to discover she truly did.

"Here, I brought you something," he said. He reached into his bag and pulled out a beautiful satin dress. It was one of Aliatta's own, the one he had stuffed into the bag before they left Earlington. "Put this on right before you are about to come upon the settlement. You will no doubt be greeted as royalty when you arrive and you may as well look the part." After a final hug, Raz turned and left the room.

Aliatta looked at the dress wryly—one more thing to carry. Then she took it in her arms and hugged it close. If it had been important enough for her brother to bring all this way, then she would do him the honor and wear it. She tucked the dress carefully into her travel bag.

By mid-afternoon, the eleven travelers were ready: Elior, Grace, and Aliatta, Levi, Ian and Rosemary, and Faran and Kamila with their children. Lady Adina took them down corridor after corridor through the castle until they came to a steep stone staircase which wound its way even further down into the mountain. It was musty and, if they listened, they could hear the sound of running water in the distance. After what felt like a long time, they arrived at an underground stream.

"This is where all of our water comes from," explained Lady Adina. "There are four streams which flow beneath our city. Each stream is connected to a well on the surface. In this way, even if we are surrounded for a long time, we will never run out of water and, it is also a way to escape, known to only a few of us. Follow this stream eastward and you will eventually emerge in the forests of the Livid. Goodbye my friends. May the High King continue to guide you in your journeys."

"And in yours," they replied.

"Lady Adina," Aliatta called as her friend turned to head up the stairs. "Do you really think you will be okay?"

"Of course," the lady said with a smile. "Didn't you see the shining lights coming down to surround the city? It would be silly of us to think we are alone in our battles." With that, Lady Adina began her ascent up the stairs, ready to take her place of service in the fight.

After one last look at her disappearing friend, Aliatta turned to follow her companions to her journey's end.

# 32

# SALEM FOREST

It was a quiet journey through the underground caverns. A soft glow of light surrounded them and continued on for several feet in front of them. Everywhere else was darkness. To their right, at the edge of the light, they could hear the sound of gently running water.

"We have company," Levi said with a smile, motioning to the light which encompassed them. The presence of an Erela was a cheering realization, one that served to lighten the mood of the whole group.

After they had been walking in silence for quite some time, the children began to get antsy, for it is a hard thing for young ones to remain quiet for an extended period of time, and their ability to do so was running thin.

Giron was the first to break the silence. "What is it like in the Valley of the Loyal Ones?" he asked.

"Do you like living there?" asked Henry, following the lead of his older brother.

"Have you always lived there?" piped up Marnie.

"Children," Kamila reprimanded them gently, "leave Levi alone.

He needs to be able to concentrate on the way we are going. You don't need to ask him so many questions."

Levi smiled, "It's okay," he said. "I would love to tell you about it. I was born there, Marnie, so yes, I have always lived there. In fact, I had never left or known anything different until I was sent to get Lady Aliatta. I love living there, Henry. As for what it's like, well, you wake up every morning to the sight of the sun streaming its light across multi-colored mesas rising up to greet the high mountains behind them. If you listen carefully, you can hear the trees rustling, the birds singing, and the river gurgling. There are people from nearly every race living and working together. Everybody has work to do before breakfast and while you eat, you talk to each other about what the High King showed you that morning—about himself, the people around you, and the world he gave us."

"It sounds perfect, almost too good to be true," stated Aliatta softly. "Why on earth did you have to leave? Couldn't someone else have come to get me?" she asked.

"I didn't have to leave. I was given the choice to go or stay. If I had said no to the task, if I had chosen to stay where I was comfortable, someone else would have been chosen to go. But I knew I wanted to serve the High King more than I wanted to remain in my own comfort. Maybe the High King knew I needed to see that there is a world in need. The world needs the peace and beauty you can experience in that valley. It is a good place to learn, to rest, to have refuge, but it isn't where the High King wants all of us to stay, at least not yet. I've now been able to see that there is a troubled world in desperate need of the things I've learned in that valley. If I keep it all to myself, where does it leave the world?"

"So, I won't be staying there forever?" Aliatta asked hesitantly.

"I don't know," Levi replied. "I don't know how the High King will lead you, but I would venture a guess that no, you won't be there forever. All I really know is that I was sent to bring you to the valley and to teach you what I've learned along the way. It is probably safe to say that you will spend many years there, until it is time for you to take what you have learned and share it with the rest of Novus, just as you shared your knowledge of reading and writing with the group in Wintertide."

The conversation continued and was a welcome change from the silence they had earlier been walking under. Levi never lost his concentration in leading them, as Kamila had been afraid he might, but seemed to grow ever more excited as they traveled. It was the kind of restless excitement one gets as they begin to feel in their bones that they are almost home.

After a couple of days, they spotted a different kind of light ahead of them. It was a natural light, the kind of light given by the sun, and not the supernatural light they had been receiving from the Erela. A short time later, they came up from the underground caverns and found themselves in a thick, lush forest. To the east, scarcely visible through the tops of the trees, majestic mountains thrust their peaks upward into the floating clouds above.

Aliatta looked around and noticed that some of the trees were not trees at all. Rather, they were tall, broad Livids. Being much larger than those of the northern forests, these Livids more closely resembled full grown redwood trees. As the group walked onto the fresh green grass, the Livids bowed their heads and rustled their leaves in respectful Livid greeting.

"Welcome, oh worthy servants of the High King," rustled one of the Livids. "Welcome to our refuge, our home that is only visible to those who have eyes to see the Truth. Welcome back, Levi, conquering servant of the High King. You are now no longer an apprentice, but have proven yourself to be a master. Welcome, Queen Aliatta. We of the Salem Forest are at your service. We have come to meet you and to accompany you on the final leg of your journey."

"Shalom. It is good to see you again, good teachers," said Levi, bowing his head in a show of respect to his old tutors, "but I'm afraid you speak too soon in regards to your words about me, for I have not yet finished my task."

"Your humility does you credit, Master Levi, but indeed, my words are not premature, for in the eyes of the High King, the moment you began was the moment you also completed. Even so, you will continue to journey with us to bring the Queen to the Valley of the Ronan. Before we begin, however, I sense you are all in need of a rest, so sit now. Rest. Eat."

The Adamas gratefully sank down onto the soft, grassy forest floor (such a nice change from the cold, wet ground they had rested on in the caverns). Once they were all settled, the Livids gave them deep wooden bowls filled to the brim with a variety of fruits and nuts.

While they ate, Aliatta engaged in a private conversation with Levi. "Why are they calling me Queen?" she whispered. She was not nearly bold enough to ask them directly. "I'm nowhere near being Queen. I don't want to be Queen! I've never wanted to be Queen!"

"Don't you?" Levi whispered back in a gentle challenge. He looked deeply into her eyes.

"Well—" Aliatta faltered. "I *didn't* want to be Queen—not when the Duke and Duchess of Earlington told me I'd been chosen to be."

"What about now?" he persisted. "What about being Queen under the guidance of the High King, rather than the Dark One?"

Aliatta paused and thought. She was surprised to discover that something within her had indeed changed. There was a desire which had never been there before. Something else began to dawn on her as well. She thought back to her grandmother's words to her so many months before—back to before she'd even known Raziela was her grandmother. *The High King promised me that one day, one of my* descendants *would help usher in a new age of light for the land,* Raziela had said. Aliatta gasped in sudden realization. Her grandmother's last words came to her again, only this time they made sense. *You are my descendant*— "That's what my grandmother meant, isn't it?" she said in breathless awe. "I'm her descendant. I'm the one the High King has chosen to be Queen so I can help bring back the light."

"Yes, the High King has chosen you, but like I did, you also have a choice. If you choose not to be Queen, then He will find another descendant of Raziela's to complete the task."

"Then, I guess—" she said slowly, "I guess, maybe, I'm willing to be that kind of Queen, as long as I have someone to show me the way."

"Well then," said Levi with a shrug, "I can only suppose these Livids call you Queen for the same reason they call me a master—in the eyes of the High King, the moment you accept and begin the journey is the moment you have also completed it."

"I'm not sure I understand," she whispered with a frustrated sigh.

"Few do," he said with a sympathetic smile. "You need to realize that the High King is beyond time. We see things as they progress from beginning to end. He sees these events, as well as all the ones in the middle, as one. Once you are among the Ronan, you will learn many more such things and, if you continue to have an open heart and an open mind, you will eventually grow to understand."

"On your feet, everyone," bellowed one of the Livids. "We still have a long way to go and it is time to get started!"

The Adamas reluctantly stood to their feet, uncertain how much more walking their bodies would be able to take. Much to their surprise, they discovered a new strength, a new energy. They walked silently at first, following the Livids south through the emerald forests and across a sparkling river via a bridge of well-placed stones. The Livids soon began to sing. It was a joyous little tune—one that made you want to skip and dance. The melody was beautiful and before long, Levi joined in the singing. Soon after, Aliatta gave in to the influence of the music and began to dance. She even took to humming along with the melody. The Livids looked at her with smiles of approval and her heart felt light at the thought of having earned the approval of such a noble people.

The Livids sang for many hours. It wasn't until they stopped to eat that the Livids ended their songs.

As they sat relaxing and eating, a thought suddenly occurred to Aliatta. "Levi," she said, "Who are the Ronan? You said I was going to be among them. Are you one of them?"

"I am," he replied, "and so are you. Ronan is simply the name given to those who are loyal and faithful to the High King. Many of the Ronan now reside in the Valley of the Loyal Ones, which is also known as the Valley of the Ronan. Most of the older inhabitants originally came from Zion, but there are people from nearly every race, from every part of Novus, there now, and as you saw on our journey, there are Ronan who still reside in other parts of the country."

"How did the first group find that valley?"

"That is a story which I think the Livids are better qualified to tell." Levi raised his eyes in question to the Livid whose trunk was serving as their backrest.

The Livid nodded and began the tale while everyone gathered close to listen.

# 33

## THE LOYAL ONES

It was a time of great trial and testing for the loyal followers of Zion. Although they were spiritually protected, their bodies were still plagued with the consequences of the choice the King and Queen had made. Every day they fought an inner battle—a battle to conquer the darkness that so desperately wanted to take control. Every day, the followers of the High King had to decide: give in to the darkness, or rely on the strength and power of the High King.

"Besides the inner spiritual battle, there was also a very present physical battle. After the Dark One's malicious deception, more and more of the High King's followers were being hunted down, day after day after day. If they were caught, they were given the brutal choice of either pledging their allegiance to the Dark One or else being sent into an endless prison. For days and weeks, hosts of Erela and a few brave Adamas would sneak back into the city for the purpose of smuggling out anyone else who still had the faith and courage to choose the High King over the Dark One. A month passed in this manner and then one day, the High King, his heart mourning over the lost city, informed them they would be making their final trek into Zion.

"'I have seen the hearts of this people,' the High King said, sadness and regret ringing through his voice. 'You will gather the last of the light on this night, before the Dark One extinguishes what little remains.'

"Everything was on schedule until the last moment. The Dark One caught wind of this final exodus and sent troops of Chashaks and Adamas in pursuit of the loyal ones who were hiding in the Qatan Forest just west of the city. At that time, only a tiny stream separated the Qatan Forest from Zion.

"The Loyal Ones could do nothing but watch in fear as the city gates opened and the Dark One's forces charged in full power against them.

"At that moment, the High King sent a powerful earthquake and a strong wind. The ground shook in a way it had never before been shaken and with a strength that has never again been matched. The earthquake tore apart the earthen barriers separating the sea from the creek. The wind sent the sea waters roaring, crashing, and tumbling through the land where the little creek lay. The rushing water widened and deepened the creek, turning it into the vast, cavernous Maarab River it is today. Zion became an island, its evil, for the time being, restricted from spreading any further by the immense water pounding against it on all sides. With all light removed from Zion, the city sank sink ever further into darkness.

"The band of Loyal Ones followed the Erela south, passing through many of the developing cities of Novus. Before long, they became known among the people as the Ronan. Most of the Ronan journeyed for many months until they arrived at the place where the High King had been leading them. Here they settled into days of peace—learning, teaching, and living out the ways of the High King. Others among those who began the southern journey chose to remain as a remnant in the cities and settlements they passed through. They were strengthened for the rest of their days by the Erela as they served as beacons of burning light among their peers."

By the time the Livid finished speaking, the Adamas were fighting heavy, sleepy eyes. Giron, Henry, and Marnie had already fallen asleep. The Livids smiled as they gently picked up the weary travelers and nestled them comfortably and securely into their branches. Then they continued on their southbound journey.

For the next several days, the Adamas alternated between riding in the branches of their Livid friends and walking leisurely beside them. The children had great times climbing in and out among the branches, something which is notably more challenging to do when the tree is moving. Aliatta found herself immersed in trying to count how many different shades of green she could identify.

"I've found fifteen!" she exulted to Levi one day.

"Not bad for a beginner," he teased.

"A beginner! How many can you count?"

"I've identified forty so far, but the Livids tell me there are at least seventy different shades of green in this forest alone."

The Livids never seemed to sleep. During the night, all of the Adamas would find themselves tucked securely into the branches. Then they would sleep while the Livids continued to walk. In this way, a journey which would have taken them at least a week was accomplished in a matter of days.

And so it was that Aliatta awoke one morning to discover that the trees of the Salem Forest were thinning out and the large mountain peaks to the east could no longer be seen towering above the tops of the trees.

"We will arrive at the settlement before noon," announced the Livid who carried her.

Aliatta nodded, but could feel her stomach twisting into knots.

"Do not worry, Queen," spoke the Livid again, sensing the tenseness in Aliatta's body and spirit. "They will welcome you as we have welcomed you."

"But what about after?" Aliatta asked nervously. "What if I fail to measure up to all their expectations? To all your expectations?"

"And what expectations might those be?" inquired the Livid.

"I don't know—to be great? To do something powerful?" It still made Aliatta uncomfortable to hear the Livids referring to her as Queen. What if she wasn't able to do the great and powerful things they were surely expecting her to do?

The Livid's voice was incredibly practical when she answered. "The first expectation," she said, "was for you to come, and you came. The next expectation is for you to learn. That is all. What is to be expected of you in the future, only the High King knows, and just as He—through your willingness to follow him—helped you meet the first expectation, so He will help you with every other task He gives you."

Aliatta relaxed—a little. She was expected to learn. That was an expectation she could handle. She sat back in the Livid's limbs and looked at the others in her company who were also riding along. Her eyes met Levi's and he gave her an encouraging smile.

"The Livid is right," he said. "The High King has been with you every step of the way. He also sent me and many others to help you along as well. With every new task, you will have exactly what you need to complete it. You will be expected to learn a great deal once we arrive, but your first task will simply be to meet the people. They will accept, love, and respect you, as we all do."

After they had traveled a little further, Levi requested they stop.

"With great respect, Master Levi," said the leading Livid, "we are about to arrive at the Valley of the Ronan."

"Exactly," Levi said with a smile. "I am coming home and I want to be able to walk the rest of the way."

They stopped and the Adamas climbed down. While the others stretched their muscles, Aliatta took the opportunity to excuse herself from the rest of the group, taking her mother and Rosemary with her. A short while later, they reemerged. Grace and Rosemary came first. Behind them walked an elegant princess, richly dressed in a blue silk gown, her hair intricately braided atop her head.

The Princess smiled, slightly embarrassed to be dressed in such finery in contrast to those around her. "It was Raz's suggestion," she said shyly.

Levi nodded in approval. "It was a good one," he stated simply. "You are a Princess and you may as well look the part."

The Livids gestured for Aliatta to take the lead, which she did, ever so hesitantly. Another dozen steps brought them out of the forest. Princess Aliatta looked down a gently sloping hill to a clearing where a little community was actively at work. A low stone wall surrounded the settlement and the echoes of joyous voices mingled with the noise of work being done. A lone voice rang out loudly above all the rest and a flurry of excited cries alerted the princess to the fact that their presence had been discovered.

Princess Aliatta began a slow, regal descent down the hill, the company of Adamas and Livids following behind her.

# 34

# QUEEN OF NOVUS

She had not yet made it halfway down when the eastern gate of the settlement opened and a long procession of Adamas, Yylecks, Zobeks, Noroks, and Pronghorns filed solemnly out.

The two groups met face to face not far beyond the settlement. For a few seconds, they stood without speaking. Then, following the lead of the man and woman who led them, the group from the community bowed themselves low in homage to Princess Aliatta.

Aliatta stared in bewilderment at the bowed bodies before her and turned to seek council from her tutor. To her even greater astonishment, he and all the others behind her were also bowing.

Not knowing what to do or how to proceed, Aliatta did the only thing which came to mind. She strode up to the man who seemed to be the leader of the Ronan, put her hands on his, and pulled him to his feet. "Please," she said, "I don't want you to think I'm unappreciative of the esteem you have just shown me. I am honored and do thank you for this show of respect, but I fear I do not deserve it. I am only a young girl and have done nothing worthy of such honor."

The wizened man was not much taller than the girl herself and he now looked her full in the face. His voice was confident and understanding as he spoke. "Not in your eyes perhaps, Princess, but then, we don't always see ourselves so very clearly. You have left the comforts of your castle and the familiarity of your home to pursue One whom you knew but little about. You received instruction and correction and walked according to the knowledge you had to the extent you knew how. You received people kindly, regardless of rank or situation. You recognized what you knew and shared that knowledge with others. But perhaps you are right in one respect, for you are still young and have much to learn. The honor we give is not only for how far you have come, but for what you may become if you continue to journey in the same way you have begun. And so we welcome you, Princess Aliatta, chosen servant of the High King, descendant of the Writer, the High King's chosen Queen of Novus."

Back in Earlington, the idea of being Queen of Novus had revolted her. When the Livids called her Queen, she had been uncertain. But now, in this place, at this time, it was a role she could really see herself accepting—someday.

The older man offered his arm to the young princess and they turned to make their way into the settlement. As they approached the stone wall, Aliatta found herself breathing easier, feeling more freedom, more peace, than she had ever felt in her entire life. She may not, as Levi had suggested, stay here forever, but for now, she was home—right where she had always longed to be—right where she belonged.

From somewhere unseen, the High King smiled and his heart rejoiced as He watched this beloved creation of his enter into his rest. Her first journey was over. Her other journeys were about to begin.

# EPILOGUE

To My Dear Friend – wherever you may find yourself,

This scroll contains the writings of my grandmother, Raziela, as well as the first part of my own journey. I have now fulfilled my grandmother's request in adding my own journey to hers. Whatever may happen to me in the future, it is my hope that through reading my story, you may grow in knowledge and understanding of the High King; that you may have eyes to see his workings in your own life.

Five years have passed since my own journey with the High King began. My days here in the Valley of the Ronan have flown by faster than I could have believed possible, but alas, they are now nearing an end. We have received word that your own dear city of Brance is once again in jeopardy. We have learned that after his failure to defeat the city nearly four years ago, the Dark One pulled his troops back and since that time, has been consumed with the task of rebuilding his army. It is now rumored that King Lev himself will be leading the troops and is at this very moment en route to Brance. The elders tell me that my time has come. I will soon be departing with a large group from this settlement to assist in the defense of that great city. If all goes well with the battle, I will thereafter take my place as Queen of Novus. I have the greatest hope of meeting you again soon. All those in the Valley send you and your family their love. May the High King live forever and his light never be extinguished.

With Great Love,

A Servant of the High King and your friend,
    Aliatta

Join the Invisible Battles community
Get free updates, special content, and
more from the world of Novus.

Join us as we prepare for the next great adventure.

**InvisibleBattles.com**